'Give me my nightie, please. It's over there.' Being cocooned in a sheet gave Sherry not the slightest sense of security, with Tyler Brennan loose in her bedroom.

He picked up the sleepshirt which, some time during the night, she had dragged off and flung away, and held it up by the shoulders, an expression of extreme distaste on his handsome features.

'What's happened to the silk nightdresses I bought you?'

'Oh, it—it's too hot out here for them,' she mumbled.

'Too hot?' He raised one dark brow in delicate disbelief. 'Silk, my dear Sherry, is the one thing—apart from her own delectable skin, that is——' his voice seemed to wrap itself around her, and as their eyes met she found herself quite unable to tear hers away '—in which a woman feels she is wearing nothing at all.'

He was doing it again, weaving a spell around her with only his voice as a weapon.

'You know something?' she said belligerently. 'I think you've got some sort of a fetish about silk.'

But he only gave her a slow smile. 'Hasn't every man?'

WE HOPE you're enjoying our new addition to our Contemporary Romance series—stories which take a light-hearted look at the Zodiac and show that love can be written in the stars!

Every month you can get to know a different combination of star-crossed lovers, with one story that follows the fortunes of a hero or heroine when they embark on the romance of a lifetime with somebody born under another sign of the Zodiac. This month features a sizzling love-affair between **Gemini** and **Pisces**.

To find out more fascinating facts about this month's featured star sign, turn to the back pages of this book. . .

ABOUT THIS MONTH'S AUTHOR

Rebecca King says: 'Being a Gemini myself, I understand all too clearly my hero, Tyler: his dual personality—moods which one instant make May-June babies euphoric and hurl them down into the pits of despair the next. Geminis are easily bored. . .impulsive. . . impatient. . .

'The most sensible thing I've ever done is marry a Taurean. My solid, dependable, feet-on-the-ground husband gives me the calm centre which I lack myself, even though on occasions I know I drive him crazy!

'I firmly believe in Astrology, but I also believe even more strongly that we shouldn't lie down under what Fate throws at us. I think sometimes, like my heroine Sherry, we have to say, "Sorry, but I want that lucky break and I'm going to make it happen."'

DOUBLE DECEIVER

BY
REBECCA KING

MILLS & BOON LIMITED
ETON HOUSE   18–24 PARADISE ROAD
RICHMOND   SURREY   TW9 1SR

First published in Great Britain 1991
by Mills & Boon Limited

© Rebecca King 1991

Australian copyright 1991
Philippine copyright 1991
This edition 1991

ISBN 0 263 77117 2

STARSIGN ROMANCES is a trademark of Harlequin Enterprises
B.V., Fribourg Branch. Mills and Boon is an authorised user.

Set in 10 on 12 pt Linotron Times
01-9105-49832Z
Typeset in Great Britain by Centracet, Cambridge
Made and printed in Great Britain

CHAPTER ONE

'OH NO.'

There was a faint but distinct ping, and from her position behind the hotel reception desk Sherry saw, across the acres of plush carpet, the light flash above one of the lift doors.

She glanced at her watch. One-thirty a.m. All the guests were tucked up snugly in their four-star beds, so—it could only be Joe Higgs, the doorman-commissionaire, bored with another long night in his cubby-hole down on the ground floor, on his way up to give her the benefit of yet another series of anecdotes on the career of Sergeant-Major Higgs. After only a month as receptionist at the Brennan International Hotel in Bristol, she was pretty soon going to be qualified to write a blow-by-blow account of every British military campaign from the Normandy landings onwards.

Still, it was only because he was so lonely since his wife had died, so Sherry suppressed the little sigh of irritation and as the lift door slid open with a soft hiss she closed the newspaper she had been reading and fixed a bright, welcoming smile on her face.

But the smile vanished almost before it had appeared and she found her hand had gone up instinctively to reassure herself that the chignon of sun-streaked fudge-coloured hair was its usual smooth businesslike self.

For the individual who had emerged from the lift was not Joe, but a much younger man.

Obviously getting his bearings, he paused fractionally as he stepped out, and looked around him. That glance, swift as it was, had, Sherry felt, taken in every detail of the enormous reception area before it skimmed across her, half hidden behind the bowl of white carnations, paused, then returned.

Next moment he was striding towards her, his long legs eating up the rose-patterned carpet. Joe, his florid face even redder than usual, was following at his heels, a leather case in each hand, and from behind the safety of the other man's back he rolled his eyes to convey to Sherry, in the secret mutual protection language of all Brennan employees, the message, 'Watch this one, he's a right bastard.'

But she did not need the graphic signal. There was sufficient warning in the man's purposeful stride, the arrogant set of the dark head on his neck, the all but insolent regard he was fixing on her as he pulled up just short of the desk, to have already set the warning bells pealing in her mind.

Hastily, she fixed another, this time wholly professional smile into place. 'Good evening, sir. May I help you?'

A pair of chill grey eyes regarded her, then he favoured her with a scowl. 'I was under the impression that it was one-thirty a.m.' The American accent seemed to underline even more the last two words with heavy irony.

'Well, yes.' The smile faded slightly but she hung on to it. 'You're quite right, sir. It is morning——'

'I assume my room is still available.' It was a clipped statement rather than a polite enquiry.

'Your—— Do you have a reservation, sir?'

'Of course I have a reservation. Do you think I'd risk landing myself in the backwoods of this God-forsaken country without one?'

Under cover of the desk one of Sherry's slim hands balled into a fist, but she only said calmly, 'What name is it, sir?'

'Kavanagh.'

She turned to the small computer screen beside her and pressed the relevant keys. 'Ah, yes, Mr Kavanagh. We were expecting you earlier this—*last* evening. But,' she glanced up to meet the Arctic-grey eyes, still fixed on her, 'I'm afraid we don't seem to have any record of your ringing to inform us that you would be delayed.'

'My New York flight was late,' he snapped. 'I tried calling from Heathrow but your goddamn switchboard was busy. You, making a long call to your boyfriend in Honolulu, maybe.'

Well, of all the nerve! Sherry felt two spots of angry colour rise in her cheeks but somehow forced herself to stand, head bent over the computer terminal while she counted to five, then said with measured courtesy, 'I assure you, sir, no Brennan International employee would use the facilities for their private purposes.'

'You reckon?' The open sneer rasped at her but she set her teeth grimly. 'Well, do I get a room or not?'

She swallowed. 'There is a slight problem, sir.'

'Do you mean *I* have a problem, or *you* have a problem?'

'Well, I'm afraid we both have,' Sherry said placatingly. 'We have two large business conventions here at the moment, and fifty-five Australian tourists arrived unexpectedly. Their coach broke down, so——'

'Listen, sweetie. I don't give a damn if you've got the entire population of the Australian subcontinent upstairs. Do I get my room, or do I go across town to the Hilton?'

Oh, yes, please. You do that, she thought silently. I'll gladly call you a cab.

Just in time, though, she remembered what Mike had told her. Always look at the suit. The slicker, the more expensive the get-up, the more likely it is that you've got a twenty-four-carat trouble-maker. And this—her brown eyes flicked down from the lean, tanned, square-jawed face, to the charcoal-grey mohair silk, the hand-stitched lapels, the perfect made-to-measure caress of the fabric against that muscular chest and shoulders—this was some slick suit.

As the man began drumming an impatient tattoo with his knuckles on the counter, another of Mike's axioms flashed into her mind. Always remember, Sherry, darling, however obstinate, obstreperous or downright objectionable the customer may be, he's always—until his back's turned, at least—right.

'Oh, I'm sure there won't be any need for that, sir,' she said smoothly. 'If you'll just give me a moment.'

Turning back to the computer she punched more of the keys, though with no great hope. There were those few rooms at the back, but they still hadn't been renovated—and with this man's no doubt hypersensitive tastes. . . Suddenly, inspiration struck.

'I'm afraid we had to let your reserved room go, but we'll be happy to offer you the Frobisher Suite for tonight—at no extra charge, of course.'

She smiled up at him but the man merely met her gaze for a moment then grunted what just might have been an, 'OK, I'll take it.'

Well, she hadn't expected him to fall on his knees in gratitude, but even so. . . She could be in an awful lot of trouble over this. Mike was always urging her to use her initiative, but if he was in one of his moods when he came on duty. . .

Reaching down the keys, she slid them across the desk to Joe, who had been a silent ally during the little battle of wills.

'If you'd like to register, Mr Kavanagh, then Joe will show you up to your suite.'

She watched as he scribbled an illegible signature and an all but illegible 'Los Angeles', then, as he put the pen down, she added politely, 'And if I could just take an impression of your credit card?'

He muttered something under his breath but fished one card out from among the sheaf in his pigskin wallet and handed it to her.

As he took it back, she said, 'Oh, and breakfast is served between seven and ten.'

He flashed her a shark-edged smile. 'You know something, *Ms* Sherida Southwell? I eat little desk clerks like you for breakfast—when I'm in the mood.'

For a second her eyes fell to the give-away white name badge with its crisp black lettering, which was pinned to the lapel of her dove-grey company business suit, but then she replied briskly, 'In that case, Mr Kavanagh, I'm glad you aren't in the mood just now.'

He gave her a long, considering look across the carnations, then without another word turned on his heel. Joe gave her a surreptitious thumbs-up, then picked up the cases and followed him into the lift. Sherry watched as the floors lit up—2, 3, 4, 5. Only when, a few moments later, the lights began to descend again did she expel a relieved gust of breath. Safely delivered.

In the morning, she'd leave a coded message to warn Jenny and the others. Some of the blame for the man's appalling behaviour could perhaps be laid at the door of fatigue, jet lag or whatever, but the rest no doubt was as deeply ingrained in that uncharming personality as those knot holes in the polished wood counter. Still, with any luck, he was a bird of passage, and would be gone in a matter of hours. . .

She expelled another breath, half anger, half laughter this time, directed at herself. Really, how she'd let that man get at her. Usually, she was so calm, unflappable, sweet-tempered even, but now. . .all she felt like doing was striding up and down the lobby, punching the air, to try and let off steam. Instead, though, she forced herself to pull up her swivel chair, sit down and reach for the newspaper she'd been reading before the interruption.

It was the local free sheet which Jenny had left when she went off duty. More for something to do than because she actually wanted to read, she began flicking through it again. Second-hand fridges. . .twelve-hand ponies. . . Renault Five, one careful lady owner. . . The TV pages for the coming weekend. . .*True Grit*. Mike had already told her he wouldn't be able to see her on Saturday evening—his mother who lived on her own across in North Wales, was playing up again apparently. At least she'd be able to get a Chinese meal and curl up with John Wayne.

She flipped the pages over until she came to the feature she was really looking for, Madame Arcadia's weekly horoscope. Her eyes skimmed down until she arrived at Pisces, her birth sign. 'Beware,' she read, 'your pliable nature may land you in difficulties.'

Oh, no. Sherry's brow creased in a little worried frown—maybe she shouldn't have made free with the Frobisher Suite so rashly, after all. 'On the other hand, a marvellous opportunity is coming your way—an exciting new job perhaps, travel, increased financial rewards; whatever it is, you must seize this chance of a new beginning with both hands.'

New job? New beginning? Sherry smiled faintly to herself. I'm afraid you're a month late, Madame Arcadia. I started my brand-new life at the ripe old age of twenty-six four weeks ago on May the first. All the same, though, the signs must still be there in her stars, and it was good to have her certainty that she'd done the right thing in taking this job reinforced.

Now for Mike's. She ran her pink-tipped nail up the column. . . 'Gemini: A trying time ahead, in the short term, at least.' Oh, dear. Not that Mike believed a word of it, of course. Mumbo-jumbo rubbish, he called it—but even so, perhaps she'd warn him. And—she swallowed hard—could the trying time possibly have anything to do with the guest now ensconced upstairs in the Frobisher Suite? If he really wasn't moving on but was planning on staying a week or more, the horoscopes of every one of the hotel employees—including her own—would have to be altered to read 'Stormy weather ahead'.

But Mike would cope; he was adept at dealing with

difficult clients. *Mike*. She said the name slowly, linger-ingly, secretly over to herself and felt a warm glow rise in her as her generous mouth curved into a smile which had just a hint of wistfulness at the edges.

It was strange really. Geminis and Pisceans didn't normally hit it off that well—air and water just didn't mix, some people said. But almost since that first day, when they'd been two newcomers together—Mike brought in as general manager, and she to join the team of receptionists—they'd seemed, almost by instinct, to draw together, forging a new boy-new girl bond, despite the differences of status.

Maybe Mike, through some quirk, was not a true Gemini. Warm, loving, loyal—not a two-timing cheat like some men born under that sign. . . Sherry's lips tightened involuntarily and, closing the newspaper, she crumpled it up and threw it into the bin.

She glanced at her watch yet again and gave another groaning little sigh. Still only two-fifteen. Upstairs, four hundred heads were laid on four hundred pillows. She gave an almost maternal smile at the picture, but then, at the image of one particular dark head, she frowned irritably. But she ought to be charitable. He couldn't help being delayed and, after all, jet lag took some people in funny, not to say downright peculiar ways. Maybe normally he was an amiable, easygoing guy—— Oh, come on, who are you kidding? she thought wryly. That one was born with all his character traits in place—rasping and provocative, arrogant and demanding.

She wondered, all at once, if Joe had escaped unscathed, or whether he too had been on the receiving end of that abrasive tongue. He hadn't come back to commiserate with her—perhaps he was on his own downstairs, licking his wounds. She'd ask him up for a cup of his favourite treacle-sweet cocoa.

But even as she put her hand on the internal phone it rang, making her jump slightly.

'My radiator's on the blink.'

'What?' As she recognised the voice, Sherry's fingers tightened convulsively round the receiver.

There was a Give-me-patience-to-deal-with-this-congenital-idiot-type sigh from the Frobisher end, then, 'My radiator cannot be switched off. If I'd wanted to spend the night in a sauna I'd have done so. Send up a mechanic.'

'I'm so sorry, Mr Kavanagh.' Sherry was recovering herself remarkably quickly. 'Our mechanic is off sick and his assistant won't be in until seven-thirty. As soon as he comes on duty I'll send him up.'

'And I suppose in the meantime I'm expected to fry.' Sherry hastily held the phone away from her ear slightly. The disembodied Mr Kavanagh was only marginally less intimidating than the slick-suited version glaring across the desk at her. 'You come and fix it.'

'Me?' Her eyes widened in shock. 'But I can't do that. Look, I'll call the doorman, and if he can't mend it we'll change your room.'

'Oh, yes, for some poky little broom closet, I suppose. I'll expect you in two minutes—or less.' And the phone went dead.

Sherry replaced the receiver with a clatter. Just who did he think she was? His personal handyman, or something, without an entire hotel to watch over? For two pins, she'd go up there and boot Mr Charming Kavanagh all round his luxury penthouse suite. And yet, maybe she ought to go, if only to try and pour oil on troubled waters. . .

The lift delivered her, all too rapidly, to the top floor. She walked along the silent corridor, her high heels sinking into the deep carpet, then saw that ahead of her the door to the suite was already open. He must have been super-confident that she'd come scuttling up like a frightened rabbit.

She paused, her hand raised to knock, and took a deep breath to quell the fluttering butterflies which were chasing each other round her stomach. But then, before her knuckles could come into contact with the panel, the door was wrenched fully open and Kavanagh stood there.

'I——' she began, then stopped.

'Well, come in, then,' he snapped, but for a long second she could only stand perfectly still, gaping as though she had been sandbagged in the solar plexus.

He had shed the suit in favour of a black silk kimono wrap, a gold-embossed dragon writhing its way across the front and sides. It left bare his tanned legs and a deep V of brown chest, flecked with tiny black hairs, while in between chest and legs—Sherry swallowed hard—was only the thinnest layer of black silk and a dangerous-looking golden dragon over an undoubtedly naked and intensely male body.

For some obscure reason she felt all at once a surge of gratitude for her own very formal dove-grey company suit, as she at last dragged her eyes away and somehow persuaded her legs to propel her past him into the suite.

'Now, which is the radiator?'

She had been determined to be briskly businesslike,

but instead her voice sounded maddeningly weak and far-away, as though she were just struggling back from a long, debilitating illness. This time, though, she did not make the mistake of looking directly at him, fixing her gaze instead on the air alongside his left ear.

'Through here.' He led her across the spacious sitting-room and opened a door at the far end. 'In the bedroom,' he added carelessly.

'Oh, I see.'

She swallowed hard again, her eyes taking in the two double beds which dominated the room. One of them had a duvet turned back and a rumpled sheet. So her picture of that dark head snug on its pillow had been correct. Just for a moment her insides gave an echo of that funny, rather disturbing little flutter again, then she crossed to the radiator, put her hand on it and withdrew it sharply with a little gasp as her palm came into contact with the searing metal.

'It certainly is very hot, sir,' she agreed, grateful that her voice was finally back to normal.

Hitching up her skirt slightly, she went down on her haunches, trying to view the controls in the far corner. But it was rather difficult to see them, for he had taken up his position leaning casually against the wall, so that she was all but having to peer round his bare legs.

Her heart began to beat faster. The other girls had warned her very seriously about the occupational hazard of getting oneself ensnared by lonely business-men whose wives didn't understand them. . .

Her mouth dry, she said firmly, 'I can't quite see the thermostat,' and to her relief he moved slightly further along the wall.

'Oh, gracious,' she exclaimed. 'It's been set way up.'

She glanced up at him over her shoulder, but he was apparently engrossed in studying the geometric blue and cream pattern of the carpet at his feet. 'But it moves quite easily.'

'Really?' His voice was bland. 'It must have jammed.'

'Yes, it must,' she replied evenly. 'And the radiator control is quite simple too, when you know how. Look—you just press down on it, then turn it a notch at a time.'

'Well, thank you, Ms Southwell. I'll remember that in future.'

Sherry gave him another swift look, but he was still gazing steadily down at the carpet.

She straightened up. 'Well, if that's all, Mr Kavanagh——'

'No, it isn't. That drape's off its runner at the far end there. The light's coming in from outside.'

She followed his pointing finger and saw that the curtain was indeed hanging off its track. Could he possibly have. . .? She swivelled back to him and just for a moment their glances held, her tawny-brown eyes dark with suspicion, his grey ones completely inscrutable.

Of course, she'd never know for certain, and it could just be another sign of the slipping standards within this once proud hotel. Maybe Mike still had some way to go before all the niggling little failings that he'd been brought in to eradicate were removed.

As though picking up her thoughts, Kavanagh said, 'Just what kind of a guy is in charge of this place, for heaven's sake?'

She felt herself swell with righteous indignation on

behalf of Mike. 'A very good one, actually,' she said hotly, then turned hastily away.

Just hang on—don't let him get to you, she thought despairingly, as she picked up a chair and carried it across to the window.

'I'm sure I can fix this for you,' she went on, in a tone as wooden as the windowsill, and kicking off her shoes with two little scuffs she climbed up on to the chair.

It should have been an easy job. After all, the previous couple of weeks she seemed to have done nothing each evening but hang curtains in the pretty little house in Clifton which she'd moved into as another part of her new life, and practice made perfect. But somehow the knowledge that a pair of steely grey eyes were watching her every move, openly taking in the outline of her slender body as she strained upwards, made her awkward and clumsy.

At last, though, the final hook was replaced, and she scrambled down and thrust her feet back into her shoes.

'Goodnight, sir.' She did not look at him. 'I hope you sleep well. Shall I hang the "Do Not Disturb" sign on your door as I go?'

'No. You can get me this.' And he thrust a piece of paper at her.

She stared down at it disbelievingly. 'But—room service ends at midnight.'

He lifted one shoulder in an elegant though insolent shrug. 'I wasn't here at midnight and I'm hungry. Knock up the chef.'

Sherry took a long, long breath. 'Chef went to bed ill earlier this evening, sir.'

He raised one black eyebrow interrogatively. 'First the mechanic, now the chef. Is the entire staff going down with bubonic plague, or is it something serious? Are you going to collapse at my feet any second? I ask myself.'

'I think you can be reassured on that count,' she said stiffly. 'I don't make a habit of falling down at any man's feet.'

'You don't?' He sounded mildly surprised. 'You amaze me. You seem exactly the sort of young woman to do just that.'

When she said nothing he went on, his voice hardening with just a touch of steel, 'Anyway, I want a steak sandwich—medium rare—and salad. I trust I've filled it in correctly.'

He held the order form out again and Sherry somehow restrained herself to take it, not snatch it out of his hand.

'I have the master keys to the kitchen, so I'll see to it myself, sir,' she said in a dead level tone, and had a moment's triumph as she saw what just might have been disappointment flicker in those pale grey eyes.

He was goading her, seeing just how far he could push her before she lost her cool. She was certain of that now—but she wasn't going to oblige him. For one thing, he didn't know it, but he was dealing with a Piscean here—long-suffering, far too easily put upon, or so her friends were always telling her, but at the same time patient, even-tempered and eager to please. So—all she had to do was draw on those birth-given qualities and she would keep on top of even this situation. . .

* * *

She removed the steak from the microwave, placed it between the two pieces of wholemeal bread and set it beside the already prepared salad. Carefully balancing it alongside the small glass with the three white carnations which she'd sneaked from the reception desk display, she picked up the tray and marched back upstairs.

He—that was how she was beginning to think of him—was lounging back in one of the armchairs in the sitting-room. As she set the tray down on the coffee-table beside him, she noticed the bottle of champagne from the suite's fridge-bar at his elbow—and two glasses.

'Sit down and join me.' He gestured towards another armchair, cosily drawn up opposite him, and, picking up the bottle, began peeling away the gold foil.

It was a royal command, not to be disobeyed on pain of death, but somehow Sherry stopped herself from leaping into the chair.

'It's very kind of you, sir, but no, thank you. I very rarely drink.' She addressed that space beside his left ear.

'Very wise.' All his attention was on the cork. 'But you can make an exception on this occasion, I'm sure.'

The cork came out with only the faintest pop—obviously a Masters Degree in opening champagne bottles, as well as in the social graces.

'I'm so sorry, sir.' And Sherry did her best to sound as though she was. 'But I'm afraid I can't drink while I'm on duty. It's strictly against company regulations.'

'And we daren't break the rules, dare we? Brennan International might not like it.' He regarded her for a moment and his mouth twisted. 'What a Miss Priss you are. Ah, well. Pity.' He shrugged, poured one glass of champagne and set the bottle down. 'God, what a day. And what a birthday. Goodnight, Ms Southwell.'

'Goodnight, sir.' Automatically, she turned to leave, then stopped. '*Birthday*? Is it your birthday?'

'Correct.' He flicked back the cuff of his wrap to glance at the slim gold watch at his wrist. 'At three-fifteen a.m.—which is in precisely five minutes' time—I enter, with no great pleasure, I may say,' his lips thinned for a moment into a harsh line, 'my thirty-sixth year.'

'Well——' Sherry found herself smiling rather shyly at him '—happy birthday.'

'Thanks.'

But he made no effort to return her smile, merely reaching for the glass of champagne and twisting it moodily round on its base.

As she stood staring down at him, all at once she felt her heart contract painfully. His black hair was ruffled and beneath his tan he looked very pale and tired. No, not tired, exhausted, his mouth set, harsh lines of fatigue etched in his face. What a terrible way to spend a birthday. Alone, far from loved ones—children? A wife? Yes, Sherry guessed, a wife; downtrodden, put-upon, but a wife none the less—in an anonymous hotel room in a city where most probably he knew no one. Sherry's soft heart was touched and she felt the ready tears of sympathy sting her eyes.

Before she knew quite what was happening, she had dropped down into the chair facing him. Her move-ment roused him slightly from whatever morose thoughts were engrossing him and as he raised his eyes she gave him a tremulous little smile.

'Perhaps I'll have half a glass, please.'

Without a word, without a flicker of a smile, he poured exactly half a glass and pushed it across to her. She lifted it, feeling the glass chill against her warm fingertips, and held it up to him.

'Well—er——' she said brightly '—happy thirty-fifth birthday.'

'And may all my wishes come true. That's what people say on such occasions, isn't it?'

He gave a wry grimace, but at least he allowed himself to clink glasses with her. Sherry took a cautious sip, gasped as the icy bubbles caught deliciously at her throat, then took another.

'Mmmm. Lovely.' She set down the glass and looked across at him, feeling that she at least should make some effort at conversation. 'Will you be in Bristol for long?'

'That depends.'

'Oh, I suppose it's how long your business takes?'

'Could be.'

Sherry fought down her irritation. If he didn't feel like talking, well, that was up to him, but she didn't have to stay here any longer. She drained her glass, set it down and put her hands on the arms of the chair.

'I'm afraid I must go. I left the desk unattended.'

'You mean, you'll be for the high jump if you're caught.'

'Well—not quite.'

At the thought of Mike, wearing his general manager's hat to give her the sack, she gave a small, secret smile, then catching Kavanagh's eye she hastily wiped it off her lips and stood up.

'Goodnight. Oh, would you sign the room service chit, please?'

He scribbled that illegible signature again, then stood up too. Reaching for his jacket, which he had slung across another of the chairs, he pulled out his wallet, extracted a ten-pound note and, as she took the chit, held it out to her.

She looked blankly from the note to him. 'What's that for?'

'Tip for room service, of course.'

She felt as though he had fetched her a stinging blow across the face. She'd been sorry for him, had a birthday drink with him—and now this. Anger and a strange sadness mingled in her.

'I-I'm sorry.' She shook her head, not looking at him now. 'Reception staff are not allowed to accept gratuities. And besides——'

'Besides?'

'I don't want your money.' And she turned on her heels, to make a dignified exit.

But before she reached the door she felt his hand close over her arm and next second he had wrenched her round to him.

'In that case, maybe you'd prefer this.'

Before she could protest, threaten, scream, his mouth came down hard on hers.

When she tried to jerk back her head, one strong hand went up to fasten in her hair, his fingers tangling in her chignon until it was brutally torn free and she felt the smooth knot disintegrate into wild disorder on her shoulders. As she struggled wildly, her hands trying to gain a grip on the slippery silk of his wrap, she felt his other arm go round to the small of her back, dragging her to him, the whole length of her soft, yielding body pressed to his hard, muscular one, so that she was powerless in his arms.

How could he? How dared he? Silently she ranted, her angry brown eyes signalling, Let me go, damn you, to his cool grey ones. But gradually, past all the anger, she was only aware of those warm, fierce yet at the same time tender lips, the moist champagne sweetness of his mouth against hers, taking her over completely, so that at last she stopped struggling, closed her eyes and leaned against him with a little sigh.

When at last he released her, she stepped back unsteadily, her eyes blank. But then, as she caught sight of herself in the full-length mirror on the opposite wall, hair dishevelled, face flushed, lips already swelling from his assault, the ignominy and the downright shame at how she had responded to him welled up in her.

Shuddering for breath, she looked back at him, and glimpsed what was surely a fleeting smile of triumph. That smile was his undoing. Furious in equal measure with herself and him, she brought her hand up and caught him a fierce blow across the cheek. It was strong enough to sting her palm red-hot, so that she winced, and he too stepped back a couple of paces under the force of it.

They regarded one another for long moments in silence, apart from her gasping breath, then without another word she turned on her heel and walked out, and this time he made no effort to stop her.

Back at reception, Sherry feverishly paced the carpet again, hugging herself to try and stifle that awful shuddering. What on earth had come over her? First of all to nearly give way to him like that, and then to hit him. Hit a guest. . . When Mike heard about this in the morning—and Kavanagh would surely make certain that he did—would he have any option than to dismiss her? And it was so unlike her—she was normally so calm, so placid, whatever the provocation. But he really had provoked her—he'd set out to, and he'd succeeded.

And what else had he set out to achieve? If common sense hadn't come to her rescue he'd no doubt have conveniently forgotten his long-suffering wife back in Los Angeles and advanced way beyond a single kiss.

Sherry groaned aloud. If only she hadn't been so soft-hearted as to join him in that birthday drink.

Birthday. . . Of course. She stopped in mid-stride. It was his birthday—June the third. Well, no wonder then if he was a two-faced, two-timing swine. He couldn't help himself. He was a Gemini!

CHAPTER TWO

SHERRY clasped her fist into her open palm and began striding up and down, up and down the lobby even faster. At last, though, she made herself go back behind her desk, sit down and take out the library book she had brought in with her. But she just could not focus on the words; they were dancing in front of her eyes.

Would this night never end? Despairingly, she flung the book back in her bag then, as she straightened up, her eye fell on the small box containing the electronic key cards which opened the hotel's swimming and leisure area.

Her heart beating rapidly, she took out one of the keys and stared at it. Dared she? The area was closed down at eleven and, in any case, for her to desert her post again. . . But surely no one else would arrive at this time of night—and anyway she'd only be gone a few minutes. Suddenly, a few vigorous lengths in that enchanting turquoise pool seemed the only possible way to calm her still ruffled nerves.

Feeling the uneasy prickle of excitement of doing something wholly out of character, she picked up the phone.

'Joe? I-I've got a bit of a tension headache. If anything crops up, could you handle it, please? I'm going to have a quick swim.'

She closed the door to the leisure area behind her,

effectively locking herself in, and made her way past
the array of exercise bikes and rowing machines
towards the pool, gleaming a soft sapphire under the
one light which she had switched on.

The blinds were already closed, screening her from
the outside and so, without bothering to go to the
changing-rooms, she took a towel from the locker,
dropped it on to one of the lounger chairs and began
rapidly shedding her clothes, before she could begin to
panic and abandon the whole idea.

When she reached her cream lace bra and pants, she
hesitated. Almost new, and horrendously expensive,
they'd been a pick-me-up treat for her just before she'd
started this job, and it seemed a shame to let the pool's
chlorine get at them. On the other hand. . . She
swallowed, then, letting this delicious, utterly novel
feeling of wickedness carry her along on its tide, she
stripped them off and, walking down the shallow steps,
launched herself into the warm water.

She completed twelve rapid lengths and, as the
tension peeled off her, felt relaxed enough to turn over
on her back and float, idly kicking the water up in little
jets behind her. Then, all at once, she abruptly stopped
splashing and went very still.

'Oh, no. I don't believe it!' Her voice rose to a
squeak of outraged terror.

As Mr Kavanagh straightened up from where he had
been standing beside the plastic potted palms and
sauntered to the edge of the pool, she hastily turned
back on to her stomach and began swimming away
from him. But through her frantic threshing she still
caught his low chuckle.

'My, my, Ms Southwell,' he drawled. 'We really do seem to be seeing a great deal of each other tonight.'

Without looking back, she could feel his gaze penetrating the sapphire water, taking in every creamy-pale contour of her slender body, and furiously she dunked herself down in the deep end, so that just her head was clear of the water.

'W-what are you doing here?' she spluttered.

'I could ask the same of you.'

He was still wearing the black kimono, and she didn't dare ask herself if he now had anything on underneath.

'Actually, the pool closes to guests at eleven,' she said, in the most controlled tones she could muster.

'But not to employees, apparently.'

'That-that's different,' she replied feebly, then repeated, 'Anyway, what are you doing here?'

'I felt like a swim before turning in. There was no one on the desk,' he added meaningfully, 'so I helped myself to a key.'

'Are you sure you didn't come downstairs to apologise?' A stranger had got hold of her tongue, making her say things she would never normally dare come out with.

He raised one dark brow in patent astonishment. 'Apologise? For what, Ms Southwell?'

'For kissing me.' Even as she said it, through clenched teeth, she felt the treacherous colour rise in her cheeks.

He shook his head. 'Honey, I never apologise for a kiss—and most women don't ask me to.'

His mood seemed to have changed completely. He

was teasing her, toying with her, as a snake played with a mesmerised baby rabbit.

'Yes—well——' she was floundering in the face of his supreme self-confidence '—I'm not most women.'

'No, I can see that.'

Casually, he went down on his haunches and trailed the fingers of one hand through the water. As he did so, the kimono fell away revealing once more the tanned chest, the tiny whorls of black hairs and, as he leaned forward, such a long expanse of tanned, well-muscled thigh that she was quite positive now that there was nothing underneath that writhing dragon.

All at once, Sherry realised that beyond her embarrassment was a very real fear. Her nerves already stretched like violin strings, she now found herself on the verge of unrestrained weeping.

'W-what are you doing?' she whispered.

'Oh, just testing the temperature.'

Across the expanse of water, his eyes met hers in a cool but unmistakably sexual challenge. Very deliberately, he removed his hand from the water and raised it to the cord knotted at his waist.

'Please. Just go away.'

Her voice trembling, she looked pathetically up at him, and all at once he seemed to tire of his snake and rabbit game.

'OK, if that's the way you want it, Ms Southwell.'

Abruptly he dropped his hand and turned away. As she watched, her skin burning with shame, he extracted her towel from among the pile of intimate female clothing, came round the pool towards her and dropped it within reach.

Quick as lightning she hauled herself out and, wrapping herself in the towel sarong-style, scurried past him. Quite unable to trust her voice, she scooped up her clothes and the phial of shower gel and made for the women's changing-room.

Before she had taken half a dozen steps, though, she felt his hand seize her by the wrist. Her pulses leaping wildly, she struggled to break his grip, but his fingers tightened remorselessly, pulling her round to face him.

Terrified that he was going to kiss her again, she put her head down, clutching her clothes to her as a fragile safety barrier, but then his other hand came up to tilt her chin, the thumb pressing into the soft flesh until her head was forced up. He gazed down into her wide-eyed face expressionlessly, as though she were just a picture for him to study, then his lips twisted.

'All right, Ms Southwell. No tears, please.'

With his little finger he gently lifted off the enormous tear that was glittering on her lashes and flicked it away. Then he released his hold on her and, with a dismissive gesture, turned away, leaving her to flee into the refuge of the changing-room.

Banging the door to, she leaned heavily against it, fighting for breath and waiting for her heart to stop its agonising thump-thump. Then, slowly straightening up, she went across to the mirror by the showers and stared at herself as though at a stranger.

What on earth had happened to her? She shook her head in bewilderment. She'd come on duty last night, neat and smart in her regulation grey gaberdine suit, white buttoned-to-the-neck blouse and little black and white bow, every shining hair in place, a discreet touch of make-up on her rather pale, delicate-featured face, ready and able to cope with anything.

Then, less than two hours ago, the lift door had opened and the appalling—no, the terrifying Mr Kavanagh had swept out of it and into her life, like a tornado through a peaceful desert oasis.

And now, confronting her in the mirror, still visibly trembling, was a woman, naked apart from a slipping towel—even though she was alone, she clutched at it— her hair, streaming wet, lying in drowned strands across her forehead and shoulders. Her face, washed clean of make-up, had a soft peony flush on its smooth skin, while her brown eyes sparkled with angry vivacity. And her mouth——But Sherry hastily forced her eyes away from her lips, swollen and pouting, as though, despite her terror, in eager expectation of another kiss. . .

She had showered and was just drying her bedraggled hair when she paused. Perhaps you've learnt your lesson, my girl, she told her other, mirror-self sternly; don't ever again do anything so stupid as to drop your guard and strip off when there's a shark on the prowl—and a shark, furthermore, who's already informed you that he eats little Piscean fish like you for breakfast.

She gave a slightly lunatic giggle, but then at the thought of Kavanagh, and of what the morning might bring, the giggle vanished abruptly.

'Hi, Sherry. Had a quiet night?'

Jenny, bright-eyed and bushy-tailed after an un-broken night's sleep, Sherry thought a shade crossly, erupted into the office.

'Oh, yes, delightful, thanks, Jen.' Her tone was ironic, but the other girl did not notice. 'Well, I'll be off, then.'

She wasn't on duty again until the following morning and was longing to drop into bed, to sleep for the whole day. As she came out from behind the desk, Mike appeared. Their glances met briefly and he gave her a brisk nod, then their eyes slid away from each other and she said carefully, for the benefit of anyone who might be listening, 'See you tomorrow, Mr Lloyd.'

'Have a good day, Ms Southwell,' he replied blandly. 'I hear the weather forecast is set fair for this evening.'

Sherry turned away and went towards the lift, her spirits lifting. That meant, in their hidden language, that he'd be able to come round to see her this evening, then. She hated this secrecy but, with the Brennan house rule of strictly no out-of-office-hours relationships so rigorously enforced, she could see that it had to be like this.

At the lift she paused. He was watching her and after a swift, surreptitious glance round, his lips pursed and he blew her a soft, quick kiss. She turned away, feeling the blush of joyous pleasure rise in her cheeks—and caught the cold eye of Mr Kavanagh, who had just emerged from the restaurant.

He was standing perfectly still, and she was quite sure that he had seen her little interplay with Mike, for he looked from one to the other, his eyes narrowing, before he walked on.

A little cloud scudded across the sun in Sherry's heart for a moment, and when the lift doors opened on the ground floor she only roused herself to step out as she became aware of curious glances from the couple waiting to move in past her. Oh, well, she wasn't going to let a scowl from that man spoil her day. In any case, she had already persuaded herself, through the remainder of the night, that he wouldn't report her—after all, his own behaviour had hardly been blameless.

And even if he did, she'd told herself stoutly, Mike would surely understand that she'd only slapped him because he'd kissed her. Oh, come off it, another niggling little voice had kept intruding, you slapped him because you felt yourself responding to him and that made you angry, didn't it. . .? But anyway, he obviously hadn't been in touch with Mike yet, and with any luck that quick scowl across the lobby would be the last she'd ever see of him.

She stopped for a brief chat with Joe's replacement on the door, commiserating over the latest assault by his neighbour's ginger tomcat on his prize gladioli, then went on out to the car park. Throwing her bag and jacket on to the back seat of her blue Mini, she got in, and was waiting to join the stream of traffic pouring into town when there was an urgent banging on the back of the car. A moment later, Jenny's flushed face appeared at the window.

'Sherry—stop!' she gasped breathlessly. 'Mr Lloyd says you're to come back.'

Mike? What on earth? Oh, no—she might have known that Kavanagh wouldn't, after all, be content to let the matter drop. As the feeling of unease deepened rapidly into one of impending doom, she obediently backed into the parking space again and got out.

'You're to go straight upstairs to his private office.' Jenny's blue eyes were round. 'Is it about that message you left us, Sherry? He looks really mad about some-thing—he nearly bit my head off when I said I might not be able to catch you.'

Funny little cold fingers were playing an arpeggio up and down Sherry's backbone, but she managed to smile reassuringly at the younger girl.

'Oh, well, let's go and see if I'm to be fed to the lions.' But her brave attempt at insouciance ended on a slightly quavery note.

At reception level, Jenny got out of the lift—escaped would be a better word, Sherry thought, watching her rapidly retreating back—then she pressed the button again and within seconds was deposited on the sixth floor.

Two girls coming out of personnel, almost colliding with her, eyed her curiously. She was probably very pale, she thought, and so before she reached Mike's office door—firmly closed—she tapped hard on her cheeks to bring the blood to the surface. Then she knocked, went in—and instantly those icy fingers of tension launched themselves into a full-blown sym-phony against her spine.

The man, who had been gazing out of the window, his head rested casually on his hand, turned slowly to face her.

'Come in, Ms Southwell, and close the door,' Kavanagh said crisply, and, somehow gathering her wits, she obeyed.

'But—where's Mr Lloyd?' Sherry glanced around the room, half expecting Mike to emerge from his inner office.

'Not here, as you see,' he replied succinctly.

'But I don't understand,' she said slowly, a faint frown forming between her brows.

'I've appropriated his office temporarily,' he went on suavely, and, as if to underline his words, sat down in Mike's black leather chair.

He gestured her to the one on the other side of the desk and she dropped into it, her legs trembling.

Now that she was seated, though, he seemed in no hurry to begin, as he gently swivelled himself back and forth in the chair, regarding her over his steepled fingertips. He was freshly shaved, a hint of sandalwood creeping enticingly across the desk to twitch at her nostrils, and fresh as a daisy—he obviously thrived on three hours' sleep a night, while she herself, Sherry thought resignedly, must look absolutely drained and exhausted in the strong morning light which was filtering in through the blind behind his head.

'Who *are* you, Mr Kavanagh? Really, I mean.' She broke the silence first. 'A Brennan executive, I suppose.'

'You could say that.'

A faint suspicion tugged at her mind. 'Is Kavanagh your real name?'

He nodded. 'Of course. Tyler Kavanagh Brennan.'

Sherry's jaw sagged. Whatever she'd expected, it wasn't this. 'You mean—you're a *Brennan*?'

'Afraid so.'

'But the name on your credit card. . .?' she said accusingly.

'Ah, well.' He spread his well-manicured hands in mock apology. 'These things can be arranged.'

'I see,' she said slowly, although there was a great deal she still did not see. 'Did Mi—the manager know?'

'He does now.' Deadpan.

He was going to sack her, that was what it was. Either Mike had refused to do his dirty work for him— or he wanted the pleasure himself. Well, just for once, she'd show a bit of spunk.

'You needn't prolong this charade any longer,' she said haughtily. 'I'll hand in my notice—now.'

'Please.' He looked pained. 'I haven't had you brought up here to fire you.'

'Oh?'

'Quite the opposite, in fact. I'm offering you a job.'

'A job?' she repeated stupidly. 'But I've already got one.'

'Another job, then.' A hint of impatience. 'A far better one.'

'But what as?'

'As my PA—personal assistant.'

Sherry shook her head slightly, in a vain attempt to clear it. This was crazy—absolutely crazy. 'But—but why me? You don't even know me.'

'Maybe not. But I saw enough of you last night— perhaps I should rephrase that,' he added smoothly, as she felt herself blush scarlet at the memory of last night's encounter in the pool, 'I learnt enough about you to convince me that we could work together. I'm certain that we'd make a good team. People tell me I'm not the easiest guy to get along with——' he actually sounded wounded and Sherry felt her lips twitch slightly '—and you, well, you took a hell of a lot of stick from me last night with no come-back. Well, almost none.'

Their eyes met as his hand momentarily went up to

caress his cheek where surely—yes, Sherry averted her gaze in horror—there was still a faint puffiness.

'In the face of everything I could throw at you, you were calm, polite, unruffled. A very impressive display. How old are you, Ms Southwell?'

'Twenty-six.'

He gave a brief nod. 'Fine. Joanne—my last PA— was too young.'

'You mean she couldn't cope?' But how on earth could he be so sure that she could?

'Well, not exactly. She—er—left my employ when we were in Geneva last week, with—how can I put it?—personal problems.'

'Problems?'

'Yes. She was enthusiastic to mix business and pleasure, and I—er—wouldn't play the game.'

'I see.' But still she didn't. Surely the Brennan males were notorious for their womanising, so how could the hapless Joanne have offended? Not his version, for sure. Perhaps she just hadn't been beautiful enough. The Brennan women never lasted very long, but they were always outstanding, even by the glossiest jet-set standards.

'I do hope you're not confusing me with my two illustrious older brothers, Ms Southwell.' His tone was dry and Sherry jumped. Could he really have been picking up her thoughts? 'I'm not quite in the same sexual league as Craig and Greg, I'm afraid, although I frequently seem to get tarred with their particular brush. In any case,' he went on smoothly, 'you shouldn't believe quite everything you read in the gossip columns, you know. Believe me, if I had a hundred dollars for every woman I'm supposed to have laid, I'd be a rich man.'

'But you *are* a rich man,' she blurted out involuntarily.

'Well, then, a very rich man,' he responded urbanely. 'And, in any case, I'd hate you to harbour the same misconceptions as the late lamented Joanne. The Brennan finances are not exactly as healthy as they might appear.'

He glanced sharply at her. 'Whether you decide to take up my offer or not, you will treat with absolute discretion what I'm about to tell you.' He paused as though to marshal his words. 'Cracks are beginning to show up in the Brennan empire—hairline cracks at the moment, but they're there. And no,' he permitted himself a thin smile, 'I'm not talking about badly set thermostats or drapes mysteriously slipping off their runners. There have been major planning errors—in effect, no forward planning at all for at least a year now.'

Sherry heard the frustration in his voice, watched as his pencil tapped against the blotter in angry emphasis.

'The tourist industry is exploding world-wide, and Brennan is stagnating on the sidelines. All we're getting at the moment is the fall-out.'

'But your father—he'd never allow that to happen, surely?'

She had been a Brennan employee for just four weeks, but she was already familiar with the formidable reputation of Jack Brennan, whose steely eyes—Arctic-grey, just like his son's, she realised now—gazed with an unsuccessful attempt at benevolence from out of the portrait which was displayed in every Brennan International hotel reception hall.

'My father's a sick man,' he said tightly. 'It's not something we spread around, or our stock on Wall Street would very soon sink even lower, but he'll never be much good again. And as for my two brothers— well, all they care about is whether the company will keep them in the manner to which they've grown accustomed for as long as they need it.'

'And you weren't involved in running the firm?' Against her will, she was becoming interested.

'No. I've always preferred to do things my own way. I broke out and started up a computer software company, and when I tired of that I set up my own electronics firm in LA.'

'But now you've been brought in?' she said slowly.

He nodded grimly. 'Or rather, brought myself in. Shining knight Tyler on his white horse, to do the all but impossible. I've sold my company—I was getting bored with it, anyway,' he said candidly. 'The kicks were in making a success of it, but now it practically runs itself. I prefer challenges—and this is one hell of a challenge. I've given myself two years to put us back on our feet, starting with this lightning familiarisation tour.'

'Spying mission, you mean, don't you?' The unwise words were out before she could stop them.

He eyed her coldly. 'What does that mean?'

'Well,' the realisation of his deception added a bitter edge to her voice, 'travelling incognito, leaving a trail of distraught porters and desk clerks in your wake. It's very easy to terrorise people who daren't answer back, you know.'

He had the grace to look slightly shamefaced. 'I admit I went a little further than I'd planned last night, but it was your own fault.'

Sherry flushed indignantly. 'Oh? How do you make that out?'

'I usually know when to call a halt before there's any real harm done, but there was something about you that got to me, driving me on to see just how much you could take.'

'And you found out,' she said tartly.

'Yes, Ms Southwell, I guess I did.' As he stroked his cheek reminiscently once more, he flashed her a swift, wholly unrepentant grin but she forced herself not to respond.

'Just supposing I took this job——' which she had not the slightest intention of doing, but she had to make her point '——I wouldn't be prepared to help you out in your play-acting.'

'Now, that's a pity. I was rather hoping that we could turn it into a make-believe husband and wife act. You know the kind of thing—only twin beds available and you, the dewy-eyed honeymooner, positively insisting on a king-sized double.'

'I most certainly would not.' As she glared at him, the infuriating colour rising to her cheeks again, he raised his arms as though in surrender.

'OK, OK, just a thought. Actually, this is my last stop-over. I'm heading back for LA tomorrow to report on my findings.'

'So where would I—I mean, your PA come into things?'

'You—sorry, *she* will generally smooth my path. See to all the fiddling little details I can't be bothered with.'

Yes, I can believe that, she thought tartly, but sensibly kept her mouth shut this time. 'There'll be a great deal of travel—negotiating with foreign governments, landowners, local businessmen and so on. Do you speak French?'

'Well—er—yes, I do, actually.'

'Great. I don't—and this time next week I'll be in Tahiti prospecting for a potential new site.'

'Yes, but——'

'I can promise you one thing, Ms Southwell. With me, you wouldn't be bored—not for an instant.'

Sherry didn't doubt it. She'd be permanently breathless, permanently in a state of collapse trying to keep up with his exuberant, tireless energy. Typical Gemini, of course—the thought leapt into her mind. Hyperefficient, hyper-exhausting for everyone around him, easily bored——'

'I, on the other hand, am easily bored.' She started again—he really must have the telepathic gifts of the true Gemini. 'So one of your main duties would be to—er—divert me.'

And just what did he mean by that? she wondered. It really was as well that she wasn't taking up his offer, because—she realised it now for the first time—on top of everything else, Tyler Kavanagh Brennan was an extremely—no, an *excessively*, attractive male. . .

'Well?' He leaned back in his chair. 'Do I take it you're accepting?'

Accepting? To travel round the world, see places she'd only dreamed of. . .to be at the centre of major decision-making. . .

'I——' She could feel herself being caught up in a whirlwind of dangerous exhilaration. What would Mike say when she——? Mike. The name was like a douche of cold water flung in her face. She couldn't leave him, she couldn't bear to.

'No. I'm sorry, but I can't.'

She shook her head, softening her blunt refusal with a smile, but he did not respond. His black brows came down in a scowl.

'So you're intent on staying a little desk clerk all your life?'

'Not necessarily,' she replied evenly, 'although I enjoy my work very much.'

'It would be quadruple your present salary,' he said casually. 'Plus a generous package, of course—dress allowance, et cetera. I've told you, I'm giving it two years. By then, you could have earned enough to set yourself up on your own. Or I might even need you in my next enterprise—whatever that might be. This really is a one in a million chance, you realise?'

Yes. She didn't need him to tell her that. Just for a moment, she hesitated again, but then said resolutely, 'I really am sorry, but the answer is definitely no.'

'May I ask why? Apart, that is, from the fact that you don't have a shred of healthy ambition in your body.'

His acid tone made her wince, but she forced herself to shrug carelessly. 'Let's just say, for personal reasons.'

'You have family commitments? A husband, children?' Somehow, he made them into dirty words.

'No, I—' She bit back the rest. She was turning down the job, wasn't she, so there was no need to reopen those barely healed wounds for his benefit?

'Fancy-free, then—like me.'

Oh. So—always assuming he was speaking the truth,

of course—she'd at least misjudged him about that mythical, put-upon wife back in Los Angeles. . .

'I suppose that means a boyfriend, then.'

He somehow made that into a dirty word too, and she felt herself blush under his narrow-eyed scrutiny. Now that she knew who he was, though, she thought desperately, it was even more vital that no hint of her friendship with Mike should get through to him.

'That's my own business,' she said stiffly.

'Maybe it is, and maybe——' But then he abruptly snapped his lips shut on whatever he'd been about to say and stood up. 'Good morning, Ms Southwell.'

'Good morning, Mr Brennan.'

Sherry scrambled to her feet and somehow made it across the room and out into the corridor. Once the door was safely closed, though, she leaned against it for support, weak with relief. Back in there, she'd almost given in—almost, as he'd whirled her dizzily off her feet, acted out of character for the second time in a few hours. Mercifully, though, she'd somehow kept her head.

But then halfway down the corridor she stopped dead, Madame Arcadia's words flashing into her mind. 'Marvellous opportunity. . .exciting new job. . .travel . . .financial rewards.'

She felt a shiver of apprehension run through her. What on earth was she doing, going against her horoscope like this? She bit her lip irresolutely. But no—this way she'd have Mike, wouldn't she? Oh, he'd have pretended to be pleased, for her sake—but it was he, not Brennan, who was offering her a marvellous opportunity to pick up the pieces of her life. And a new, loving relationship was far more important than a new job, however glittering that job might be.

So—sorry, Madame Arcadia. I hope you understand.

CHAPTER THREE

'YOU idiot, Sherry.' Mike, who had been lounging back on her chintz sofa, straightened up with an incredulous laugh. 'What the hell did you do that for?'

'But Mike——' Shocked, she stared at him.

'You realise you're turning down a one in a million chance?'

Sherry stiffened. Hadn't she heard those exact words from another pair of lips just hours before? The image of a dark, unsmiling face shifted across Mike's for a second, blotting out his fair, boyish features, until she thrust it away, her lips tightening. She had, after all, slept only fitfully through the day, waiting for Mike to arrive, longing to tell him her news. And now. . . Her spirits were dropping as fast as a lead plumbline.

With a nervous gesture, she smoothed back her long fair hair, now hanging loose round her shoulders, then got up precipitately and went across to stand looking out of the window.

'I thought you'd be glad I'm not going, Mike,' she said in a low unsteady voice.

'Oh, sweetie, of course I am—for my sake, but I was thinking of you.'

She heard him get up, then a moment later he put his arms around her. She turned in his embrace and smiled up into his pale blue eyes.

'Don't mind me.' He pulled a face. 'It's been quite a day.'

'With Brennan, you mean?' Her voice actually managed to sound natural.

He nodded. 'Yes, he's been giving me one hell of a time—going through everything with a fine-tooth comb. It's just as well he couldn't find anything to quibble about,' he added with a hint of self-satisfaction, 'or I have the distinct feeling that yours truly would have been out on his neck by now.'

'Oh, poor love,' she said sympathetically.

'And I gather from Joe that you had quite a night with the bastard, too.'

'Mmmm.' She could not trust herself to elaborate, conscious that Joe scarcely knew the half of it. If Mike should discover that Brennan had dared to kiss her, company employee or not, he'd——

'Sherry,' he murmured huskily.

She gave him another tremulous smile, then felt his fingers tighten on her arms.

'Darling, don't send me away tonight.'

Sherry tensed. She loved Mike, didn't she? So, in that case, this was what she'd been waiting for.

'You've been very cruel, my sweet, pushing me away every time, but you won't tonight, I know,' he whispered in her ear, and began making little nips at her lobe.

Desperately, Sherry willed herself to surrender, but next moment that something very deep inside her which wouldn't go away made her turn her head sharply.

'No, Mike.'

Now that the moment had come, she knew that she still wasn't ready to make that final commitment, opening herself to the risk of cruel betrayal again. And yet, why should she fear that with Mike? He was so different. All the same, as his lips slid down the side of her throat, she felt a faint shudder, almost like revulsion, run through her.

'No, Mike,' she said again.

'Why the hell not?' He scowled at her. 'Are you frigid, or something?'

'No.' Fleetingly, the memory came to her of her body's treacherous response to that other kiss. 'I-I mean, I'm just not ready,' she whispered miserably.

'Well, it's time you were, for God's sake. I've been a damn sight too patient already. You know how much I want you.'

He pulled her to him with one hand, while the other slid under her pink T-shirt to fasten over her breast, his fingers kneading painfully at the soft flesh. She tried to back away, but only fetched up against the windowsill.

'No, don't,' she said frantically.

'*Yes*, Sherry.'

But then, as the doorbell pealed loudly through the little house, he cursed and loosed his grip slightly so that she wriggled free.

'Don't open it. They'll go away.'

'Yes—yes, I must.'

Breathlessly, she went through to the hall and flung open the door.

'Good evening, Ms Southwell.'

Her jaw sagged open in a combination of disbelief and horror. Tyler Brennan, encased now in narrow-legged grey cords and a pale lemon sweatshirt, was leaning against the frame, gazing out across the gorge of the River Avon, apparently admiring the graceful lines of Brunel's suspension bridge silhouetted against the June evening sky.

'Quite a view you have on your doorstep.'

Sherry goggled at him. A sound which might have been 'yes' came out of her mouth, then somehow she pulled the bits of herself together.

'What do you want?'

He clicked his tongue reprovingly. 'Now, that's what I call a really warm English welcome. Aren't you going to ask me in?'

'No, I'm not,' she blurted out and went to slam the door in his face.

Lazily, it seemed, he put up a strong—extremely strong—hand against the blue-painted panel, and two seconds later—she was not quite certain how—he was standing beside her, his tall, muscular frame somehow incongruous and very masculine in her dainty hall.

'*Please*—just go away,' she begged him in an undertone.

But then, despairingly, she heard Mike call, 'Who was it, Sherry, darling?' and a moment later he appeared.

If her nerves had not been racked to screaming-point, his face might have been comic. As it was, she saw the two men frown at one another and leapt in hastily.

'Mr Lloyd just called to drop something I left at work,' she babbled.

'Oh, yes,' Brennan said very pleasantly, but as his gaze ranged over her, she all at once became conscious of her dishevelled hair and, looking down, saw that her T-shirt was still hanging loose where Mike had dragged it from her jeans.

A pair of cold grey eyes—*very* cold, and Sherry shivered suddenly, though she couldn't have said exactly why—watched her as, scarlet-faced, she thrust the shirt back into her waistband. Then, with his advantage of being a head taller, those same eyes gave Mike a long, searching look.

Finally, ignoring her, he said curtly, 'I want a word in private with Ms Southwell.'

'But——' Sherry bridled.

'So, if you've no objections, Mike?'

'Er—no, of course not.'

And, before she could protest that she had plenty of objections, Mike had picked up his jacket.

'Well, goodnight—Tyler, old man.'

Brennan grunted something in reply, then turned to Sherry. 'I'll go on in and make myself at home, shall I?' and walked towards the sitting-room.

'Yes, you do that,' she snarled at his retreating back, then, as the door closed behind him, she swung round on Mike. 'How could you let that—that swine boss you like that?'

'Precisely because he is the boss.' Mike's normally good-natured face was hard. 'I intend to get right to the top in Brennan, so whatever that bastard,' he jerked his thumb at the closed door, 'wants is OK by me.' He opened the front door. 'Take care.'

Don't leave me—I can't face him on my own, she begged silently but then watched as he went quickly down the steps and crossed the road to his car.

She paused in the sitting-room doorway. Brennan had taken up residence on her sofa, leaning back with every appearance of ease, his long legs stretched half-way across the hearthrug. There was nothing on *his* conscience, she thought bitterly, and all at once she felt choked with anger, for Mike even more than for herself.

'How dare you?' she exclaimed.

'How dare I what?'

'Turn out my guest, without a word to me.' She still spoke from the doorway. It was strange; this was her own house, but she felt a sudden nervousness of advancing any further into the room. 'Does it make you feel good inside?'

'Does what?' He raised one questioning eyebrow.

'Humiliating people—making them jump through hoops at the snap of your fingers, because they're frightened of you.'

'But *you* aren't frightened of me, are you, Ms Southwell?' Behind his eyes there was a glint of humour, which angered her even more.

'No, I'm not.' She was lying, of course.

'That's good.' He nodded approvingly. 'I just like my women to have a healthy apprehension of me.'

'I thought you said you were different from your two brothers.' There was a completely new snap in her voice. 'There's an unedifying article about the oldest one—what's he called——?'

'Craig.'

'—in that magazine over there. And besides. . .' too late, she realised that she should really have responded with outrage to his casual words '. . . I'm not your——'

'Oh, come and sit down.'

He gestured impatiently towards the cushions besides him but instead she perched on an uncomfortable upright chair, as though she were the unwanted guest.

'Anyway,' she said reluctantly, 'what is it you've come for? If you're asking me to change my mind——'

'Let's just say I was curious to see what the big counter-attraction was.'

He glanced casually round the attractive room, taking in the Provençal prints in sea-washed shades of green, the turquoise and olive Indian rug, and. . .she watched his eyes as they drifted across the pine shelves which held her collection of glass and china fishes.

'And you think you know now—to your satisfaction, that is?'

'Oh, yes.' Abruptly, his gaze came back to her, and his expression was so chilly that Sherry felt the temperature in the room plummet to near zero. 'The question is,' for a moment she was astonished to see now in his eyes, as they rested on her, a softness that seemed almost like compassion, 'what's to be done about it?'

'Look.' She let out an unsteady breath. 'I'm sorry, Mr Brennan——'

'Tyler.'

'Tyler, then. You must please understand that I meant it when I said no.' She spoke placatingly. After all, she owed it to Mike to keep Tyler Brennan sweet, and besides—you might hate a Gemini, but you could never dislike them for long. And there was something about this Gemini. . .

'I'm very flattered, of course, but, well. . .' She subsided into silence but as he only gazed at her unhelpfully, she went on, 'I'm sure it would be a disaster, for both of us.'

'Oh? In what way?'

'Well——' she was floundering even more '——for one thing, you're a Gemini.'

'A what?' He stared at her in genuine astonishment.

'A Gemini. You know—your star sign. And, with my being born under Pisces——'

He gave an incredulous laugh. 'A modern young woman like you—you don't seriously go along with all that garbage, do you?'

'Yes, I do, actually.'

'Good grief. Any time, you'll be offering to read my future in my tea leaves.'

'No, I don't believe in that,' she said earnestly, 'but astrology—that's different. It's been practised for thousands of years and it really does seem to work. It's amazing how often a person's character matches up with their birth sign. Not always, of course——' she thought momentarily of Mike '——but you, why, you're an archetypal Gemini.'

'Oh, and what might that be?'

'Well, only from what I've seen of you, of course. . .' she was cursing herself inwardly for letting her tongue run away with her, '. . . I'd say that you're restless, unpredictable, easily bored. After all, you admitted that yourself, didn't you?'

When he nodded grudgingly, she went on, 'You're creative, always thirsty for new ideas, but you're also impatient with lesser mortals, moody——' He raised his eyes to fix her with a look and she swallowed, but after all he had asked her, hadn't he?

'And presumably you've got all the lowdown on my love-life,' he said sardonically.

'Well—that can be pretty complicated,' she replied non-committally.

'Tell me more.'

'I'm sure you Geminis all set out with the best of intentions,' Sherry hedged.

'So?'

'And it's just because you're born under the dual-personality sign. So you really can't help it if most of you are—two-timers.'

As she blurted out the last word, he eyed her thoughtfully. 'Forgive me, but do I detect just the faintest hint of personal experience behind that bitter tone?'

In her lap, Sherry's hands clenched convulsively on each other. 'No, of course not,' she said woodenly. 'And anyway, not all Geminis are like that.'

'Thanks.' He eyed her again. 'And does that complete your character assassination?'

'Well.' She remembered that breathless feeling, the sensation of being helplessly swept away by a tidal wave, when he'd offered her the job. In for a penny, in for a pound. 'I think living in close proximity with you would be like permanently riding a switch-back at a fairground—or the wall of death,' she added daringly.

When he laughed out loud, she demanded, 'Well, am I right?'

'Could be.'

'There you are, then,' she wound up triumphantly. 'As I said, I'm a Piscean and it's well known that most of us just can't get along with Geminis. You're ruled by Mercury, but our planet is Neptune—air and water, they just don't mix. We'd spend most of our time fighting, I'm sure.'

'Ah, but what would we do the rest of the time, do you think?'

She had been laughing across at him, but at his words the smile of triumph faded from her lips. As her breath caught in her throat, something intangible hung in the air between them, and to break free from it she leapt to her feet.

'W-would you like a drink?'

'That would be very nice.' But his voice too sounded not quite natural, and gratefully she shot off to the kitchen.

'I've got whisky,' she tilted the remnants of her Christmas bottle, 'gin,' well, there was enough for one small tot, 'and lager,' she called, then almost jumped clean through her skin as from just at her elbow Tyler said,

'A lager would be great.'

Next moment she nearly leapt out of it again as he added softly, 'Thank you, Sherry.' He repeated the name, lingeringly, so that it almost became '*chérie*'. Then, 'You know, it's the perfect name for you. Your eyes, soft, tawny—they're the colour of the finest Oloroso.'

For a few seconds, their gazes met over the open fridge door, then she snatched out a couple of cans, slammed the door shut and turned away to reach down glasses and a packet of cheese biscuits, while all the time her pulses hammered, her lungs hurt as though all the breath were being slowly squeezed out of them.

'It—it's such a lovely evening. Shall we have this in the garden?'

'Love to.'

He followed her out of the back door and down a

flight of stone steps to where a small wrought-iron table and two chairs stood on a little patch of overlong grass. They sat down and as she snapped open the cans and poured their drinks he looked around him.

'This is very pleasant. A green oasis.'

'Well,' she pulled a face, 'I call it a garden but really it's just a back yard.'

None the less, she felt a tiny glow of pride as she glanced round at the shrubs and creepers, which were bursting into lush growth on the whitewashed walls that surrounded them on three sides. An old honeysuckle spread sweetness on the warm evening air, while below it were the night-scented nicotiana and mignonettes which Sherry had planted as soon as she moved in.

'I hope to improve it gradually,' she went on. 'It's the first garden I've ever had, so I suppose it's sensible to start small.'

'Did you put in that witch-hazel and the choisya?'

'Yes. They both need a sheltered spot, so they should be fine here. The man at the garden centre said if I'm lucky they'll both bloom next winter.' She turned to him. 'You know about plants?'

He grinned. 'You sound surprised.'

'Oh, no—well, it's just that——'

'That an archetypal Gemini like me never settles in one place long enough to put down roots. Is that it?'

She laughed. 'Well, yes. Something like that, I suppose.'

'My grandmother has always been a keen gardener. I guess I imbibed some of her knowledge without realising it.'

'You grew up with her?'

'She was always around,' he said briefly.

'So you were a close-knit family?'

Something was impelling her to probe into Tyler's background, to discover perhaps what it was that made him tick.

But all he said was, 'No more than most,' then, with one of those mercurial changes of mood she was rapidly getting used to, he drained his glass and stood up. 'Thank you for the drink, but I must go—I've still got some business to tie up back at the hotel.'

'Oh, must you?' What was she saying? She really shouldn't try to dissuade him—it was horribly disloyal to Mike. But it was no use; she simply couldn't hang on to her enmity. 'I mean—business on your birthday evening?'

'Good grief. I'd completely forgotten.' And to Sherry, too, it seemed aeons ago that she had shared that birthday champagne in the Frobisher Suite. 'But I'm afraid so, yes. I'm leaving tomorrow, remember. Sherry——'

'Y-yes?'

He hesitated for a moment, but then said, 'Oh, nothing,' and, turning abruptly, left her to follow him back up the steps.

In the narrow hall, they stood facing one another, a hand's breadth apart, then, quite without warning, he lifted a strand of her hair as it lay on her shoulders and let it fall gently through his fingers.

'You should wear your hair down more often,' he said softly and, her eyes still fixed to his, she could only fumble blindly for the door-handle.

For the second time that evening she stood on the doorstep watching a man clatter his way down the steps. Tyler, though, didn't seem to have a car; he loped off in easy, swinging strides until he was hidden by the curve in the road.

She closed the door and leaned up against it, frowning with bewilderment. Something had gone terribly wrong. After the way he'd behaved the previous night, after the way he'd dismissed Mike as if he were a bellboy—what she should have done was snap his head off three times over. Instead, they'd sat companionably drinking and talking and laughing as though they'd known each other for years.

Rather thoughtfully, she went back to the garden and put the empty cans and glasses on to the tray. Instead of going indoors, though, she sat down again, still frowning abstractedly at the grass at her feet and letting the sensuous intoxication of the honeysuckle weave itself around her, until the oblong of light which fell across the very top of the wall turned molten orange from the setting sun.

'Morning, Jen. How's things?'

Sherry gave the other girl a warm smile. Another lovely morning—in spite of the early rush-hour snarl-up, she'd actually found herself whistling tunelessly as she drove down in to the city.

'Oh, Sherry, it's awful.'

She realised with a start that the girl's eyes were brimming with tears, and she felt a slight *frisson* of unease prowl around the edge of her sunny temper. Much more of this and she'd begin to lose her bubbling enthusiasm for coming in here each day.

Putting her arm round the other girl, she said gently, 'Is it that boyfriend of yours? I've told you——'

'No. It's Mr Lloyd.'

'Mike—Mr Lloyd?' That unease sneaked a little closer. 'What's the matter with him?' Her throat dry with fear, she said sharply, 'Has he had an accident?'

'No, he's upstairs clearing his desk,' Jenny wailed. 'He's been fired.'

'What?' Sherry dropped the bundle of unopened letters she had just picked up, scattering them unheeded all over the office floor. She must have misheard. 'Did you say Mr Lloyd's been sacked?'

'Yes—just like that. It's all over the hotel. That man in the Frobisher Suite—the one you warned us about—he's a Brennan.'

'Is he really?'

Sherry was holding herself in with a huge effort, but behind her stony face her brain was a maelstrom. Noticing the mail at her feet, she stooped and gathered it up clumsily.

'And he's only been here a month. I don't know what he can have done wrong.'

'No, neither do I.' Sherry spoke almost absently. She pushed the letters across to the younger girl. 'Do me a favour, Jen. Deal with these. I-I've got something I must do.'

Mercifully, she was alone in the lift all the way up to the sixth floor. She stood motionless, staring at her hazy reflection in the metal panels and thinking, The swine, the absolute swine. She and Mike had broken the company's rule about close friendships between employees, she knew that, but it was the underhand way Brennan had set about it. I've still got some business to tie up back at the hotel. He'd probably already made up his mind as he'd sat chatting in her garden. Traitor. And she'd actually liked him—just for those few minutes. . .

The door was closed, the red 'Do not enter' light illuminated. She tried the handle but it was locked.

'Mike.' Oblivious now of anyone who might be within earshot, she knocked.

'Get lost!'

'Mike, it's me. Please—open the door. I wanted to tell you, I'm handing in my notice as well.'

'Oh, go to hell, you stupid little bitch. It's all your fault.'

Sherry stared at the door panel disbelievingly. Then, as her hand flew to her mouth, she gave a tiny whimper of pain.

'Oh, Mike.' It was a heartbroken whisper and as she turned away she felt her eyes sting with tears.

Both lifts were on the ground floor and so as, temporarily at least, misery was succeeded by cold, righteous anger, she headed for the stairs and strode down to the next floor.

Outside the Frobisher Suite, she paused just long enough to dab at her eyes, then knocked. It opened immediately. Almost, she thought involuntarily, as though he'd been expecting her. She marched straight in past him, head high.

The sitting-room was untidy, and through the open bedroom door she saw a case open on the unmade bed, clothes piled around it.

'So—cutting and running.' She swung round to face him. 'You sneak in, stir up as much trouble as you can, and now you're off. You really are——'

'We'll omit the insults, if you don't mind,' he cut in

coldly. 'I've got a plane to catch. What is it you want, Ms Southwell?'

'First, to tell you what I think of you. And second to hand in my resignation, as of this minute. You lot make me sick, you know that? You're a Brennan, all right. Oh, you may not make the gossip rags, the way most of them do, but scratch a Brennan—any Brennan—and what do you come up with?'

'I don't know, but no doubt you're going to enlighten me.' The words fell into the air like chipped ice.

'A swine—a two-faced, unscrupulous swine, that's what. You sat in my garden last evening, and all the time you were plotting this.' At his treachery, a stab of pain went through her and for a moment she was choked into silence, before she went on, 'You lot always behave exactly as you want to, and then just because a manager chooses to get friendly with a lowly desk clerk—and that's all it is, an innocent friendship——'

'Really? I only have your word for that,' he said unpleasantly.

'Yes—really,' she yelled at him. 'But you're all so dirty yourselves, you're no doubt expert at digging up imaginary dirt on your staff.'

'I don't deal in imaginary dirt—and in any case I didn't have to this time.'

The contempt in his voice made her wince. 'Of course you did.'

His wintry eyes narrowed. 'I wonder. Up to now, I've been giving you the benefit of the doubt. I'd got you down as a naïve little innocent, but maybe——' He paused.

'M-maybe what?' That prowling unease had come closer still.

'Maybe you know quite well what's going on, and if not perhaps you've chosen to stay ignorant of the facts.'

'What facts? That you've taken against Mike?'

'No.' Something in his face frightened her into silence, and she flung up her hands, as though to ward off evil. 'For instance, that he has a wife and three young children living in North Wales.'

In the sudden silence, the words seemed to ripple round the room like pebbles dropped into a pool.

'I don't believe you,' she said at last. 'You're lying.'

'Well, I don't happen to have a copy of the marriage certificate about me, but I assure you it's the truth.'

But it couldn't be. She wouldn't let it be. Because if it was, her trust, which she'd been rebuilding so painfully one brick at a time——

'Still, if you prefer,' he walked over to the phone, 'I'll have Lloyd up here and you can ask him yourself.'

The unease crystalised into certainty and pounced. '*No.*'

A sob welled up from deep inside her, and she clapped both hands to her mouth, struggling for composure. But it burst out with a terrible tearing sound, as though something living were being wrenched in two.

'Oh, Sherry.'

The voice sounded angry. She heard the words as though from a long way away, then someone was taking hold of her by the shoulders, turning her to him, enfolding her in a strong, comforting embrace.

She wanted to cry. More than anything in the world,

she wanted to cry, but if she shed one single tear she'd crack completely, and then her humiliation would be complete.

Very carefully, she disengaged herself and stared up at him dry-eyed, just a faint furrow between her brows.

'Are you all right?' he asked roughly. 'Sit down.'

'No, thank you.' She managed a spectre of a smile. 'I'm fine.'

He moved away towards the fridge-bar. 'Let me get you a drink, a brandy.'

'*No.*' If she tried to swallow anything, she'd be sick all over this expensive Brennan-owned carpet.

Sherry bent down to retrieve her bag, which had slid unheeded through her fingers. She'd have to leave her job, of course. It would soon be all round the hotel about her and Mike—these things always got out, and her bruised spirit couldn't bear the shame.

She'd have to get away—away from the hotel, away from Bristol. She wouldn't stop running until she was the other side of the world——

This time next week I'll be in Tahiti. . . Her eyes flew to Tyler and she saw that he was watching her intently.

No, no, Sherry, her sensible, self-preserving self was screaming in her ear. Don't do it. How can you even think of entrusting yourself to him—yet another Gemini? Mike has shown himself for what he is—a true Gemini, after all—and this man too will take your trust and then destroy you.

And yet. . . He'd made it crystal-clear that he had not the slightest intention of getting involved in any emotional entanglements. So, she was perfectly safe, wasn't she?

She cleared her throat then, with a terrible certainty that she was doing something totally irrevocable, said, 'That job of yours——'

'Yes?'

Was there, fleetingly, a spark of triumph in those grey eyes—and, even more fleetingly, something else?

'Is the offer still open?'

He glanced at his watch. 'For the next three minutes—yes.'

'In that case,' she swallowed again, 'I'll take it.'

CHAPTER FOUR

SHERRY smiled her thanks to the waiter as he set down in front of her the dish of exotic kirsch-soaked fruits, but then, as her glance fell on the two men seated opposite her, the smile slipped slightly.

All through the meal they'd virtually ignored her—although that shouldn't have surprised her for from the first moment that morning when Tyler had introduced her as his personal assistant the two Tahitian businessmen had all too obviously dismissed her, with knowing looks, as his personal bimbo. An ageing bimbo no doubt, she'd thought wryly, but a bimbo none the less, and all through the day's tour of inspection of the tiny island which Tyler was considering as the site of the future Polynesia-Brennan hotel they had directed the whole of their highly polished sales pitch at him, with scarcely a word tossed in her direction.

She knew that she ought to be resentful, but tonight, after a superb gourmet meal, with the strange, utterly new scents of tropical flowers wafting into the candlelit hotel restaurant from the warm, balmy darkness beyond, and the gentle whisper of the sea as it ran up the pale sand almost at their feet, she could only feel the bubbling excitement that had gripped her from the moment they landed in Bora Bora.

In any case, being ignored was giving her, for almost the first time in seven days, the chance to draw breath—and a very long breath it needed to be. . .

Back in Bristol, she'd tried to insist that Tyler went on ahead to Los Angeles but he'd refused. At least, though, he'd grudgingly accepted that she couldn't possibly tie up all the loose ends of her life in three minutes flat, had cancelled his flight and at the same time booked them both on the first available plane out the following morning.

He'd gone with her to the bank, where she'd arranged for the mortgage payments on her house to be maintained over the next two years, but when she'd attempted to change the sterling in her account into dollars he'd put a hand on her arm and said firmly, 'That won't be necessary.'

Despite her protests, he'd come back with her to the house, watching impatiently as she carefully locked all the windows and almost exploding with exasperation while she emptied the contents of her fridge-freezer and took them round to her elderly neighbour. He'd even stood over her as she set about throwing her clothes into cases and had finally slammed down the lids with a 'That's plenty—a brand-new job, you're going to need brand-new outfits.'

Just once, as the jet taxied along the runway at Heathrow, a spasm of panic had taken hold of her. What on earth was she doing—or rather, allowing to be done to her? As the plane lurched and lifted, along with the ground her previous, well-ordered existence had seemed to be retreating as though she were viewing it through the wrong end of a telescope. Stop the plane—I want to get out, she'd thought inwardly. But then, catching Tyler's eye, she'd subdued the panic and buried her nose in the paperback she'd bought at the airport bookstall. . .

And then Los Angeles. . . Tyler had made her sit alongside him in the huge wood-panelled room when he reported back to the Brennan board. She'd met various top Brennan executives—and various Brennans, including the dreaded Craig and Greg. They'd been charming to her, both of them—in fact, when she thought about it afterwards, far more so, surely, than their younger brother could ever be.

He'd also dragged her down to the Beverly Center and set about buying her what seemed an enormous quantity of clothes. When she'd argued that she didn't need nearly so many, and anyway she'd far rather choose them for herself, he'd merely scowled and said that as long as she was his PA she dressed to please him.

As a last port of call, he'd swept her into a small, exclusive lingerie store where he proceeded to purchase an array of beautiful lace-encrusted silk underwear. And this time, when she'd protested in a frantic undertone that she didn't need any of it, finally pointing out despairingly that, as he never mixed business with pleasure, it surely didn't matter to him what she wore under her clothes, he'd given her a long look, then that maddeningly smooth smile and said, 'I just like to be certain that all Brennan employees are suitably dressed from the skin outwards.' And she'd submitted ungraciously.

Later, though, when at last she was alone, she'd opened the glossily wrapped packages and held them up in front of her and she'd been unable to stifle that unnerving little shiver of sensuous excitement which rippled right through her. . .

And then Tahiti. . . By that time, she'd been tottering, though whether from a surfeit of jeg lag or of Tyler Brennan she wasn't sure—the latter, she suspected. But in fact they'd scarcely set foot on Tahitian soil—or rather the tarmac of Tahiti-Faaa Airport—and received the traditional welcoming *leis* of frangipani around their necks, the pretty Polynesian girl giggling and standing on tiptoe as Tyler ducked his tall frame to receive his, before they were through immigration and Customs and on the internal Air Polynésie flight for Bora Bora.

When she'd queried, 'But I thought we were going to Tahitit?' he'd grunted,

'Well, we've been, haven't we?' Then, 'And anyway, the island I'm thinking of buying is off Bora Bora—surely I told you that?'

'No, you didn't, actually,' she'd replied tartly before turning away to gaze down at the aquamarine sea wrinkling far below them. He couldn't help himself—she must keep telling herself that. It was the Gemini factor which made him so utterly infuriating. . .

The waiter was hovering unobtrusively at his left shoulder.

'Excuse me, Mr Brennan. Telephone call for you, sir.'

Tyler pushed back his chair and with a brief nod at them all left the table. Sherry found herself watching his retreating figure, the muscular back and long, lean thighs enhanced by the pale cream linen suit. That loping, easy walk of his, graceful as a panther, sexy——

Horrified, she hastily withdrew her fascinated gaze and let it sweep round the restaurant, the soft candle glow gleaming from the tables set among the white lattice work, the violet bougainvillaea almost black against the night sky. What a beautiful, out-of-this-world place it was. 'I always like to suss out the opposition from the inside,' Tyler had told her. 'It's the most exclusive hotel by far in French Polynesia.' And as her eyes had opened wide he'd added casually, 'Until the Brennan is built, that is.'

Opposite her, the two men were deep in conversation—French conversation. She caught the eye of one of them and, more to be polite than anything, smiled and opened her mouth to make some trite remark in French about the hotel, but he had already turned back discourteously to his companion.

Oh, well. She sipped her fragrant coffee and leaned back in her chair, looking round her at the other diners. Those two women at the next table—glossy, hand-polished—surely those were Paris models they were wearing.

How right Tyler had been to insist on those horrendously expensive outfits. With a secret little smile she smoothed down the blue-green skirt of her dress, revelling in the way the fine silk caressed her thighs and stomach. Tyler had seemed to know intuitively that the soft sea shades of blues and greens were her favourites. He certainly had an eye for women's clothes. . . He must have chosen a lot in his time——

For some reason, that little thought jarred very unpleasantly, and she turned her mind away, back to the laughter and the talk around her. Idly, almost without realising, she began half listening to the two men's voices, lulled by the soft French accents. But then, as her mind finally snapped to attention, she went very still. . .

'Sorry about that.' Tyler slid into the seat beside her. 'A call from LA—from home.'

'Your father?' Sherry asked involuntarily.

'Yes. Oh, don't worry,' as she gazed at him in alarm, 'he's OK. Wanted to know whether I'd got the deal sewn up yet. After all, I've been here nearly twenty-four hours.' He flashed a grin at the men and leaned forward away from her. 'Now, where were we. . .?'

What could she do? Panic gripped her. If she threw a faint, he might only hurl the contents of the water carafe over her and have her carried away. But somehow she had to stop him.

'Er——' she began tentatively, and they all swung round to look at her.

'Oh, sorry.' Tyler grimaced. 'You look all in, Sherry. You go off to bed, and leave us to get on. *Yes*,' as she tried to protest. But he'd shown her what to do.

'I'm all right, Tyler,' she said softly, putting her hand on his arm and fluttering her lashes seductively. 'But—I would like to go to bed now.'

He looked blankly down at her hand then up into her face, as though she had suddenly, without warning, gone totally insane. Leaning towards her, he hissed, 'What the hell's got into you?'

'Please, darling.' She made a pouting little moue. 'I'm tired of boring old business. No more tonight.'

And as, out of the corner of her eye, she saw the two men exchange glances, she kicked him sharply on the ankle bone.

Tyler winced. He gazed at her, his grey eyes gleaming in the candlelight, but then they narrowed and he said, 'OK, sweetie, you win.' Turning to their companions, he threw them a wry shrug and a you-know-what-women-are grin. 'We'll finalise the deal at your office in the morning. Eight-thirty suit you?'

One of them leaned forward as if to draw him back and Sherry leapt to her feet, clutching on to his hand so that he had to get to his feet too.

'Goodnight.' Lavishing a dazzling smile on them both, she turned and began weaving her way through the crowded tables.

In the doorway, Tyler stopped dead. 'Would you mind telling me just what the hell——?'

'Ssh.' She threw a swift glance over her shoulder. 'They're watching us. Put your arm round me.'

'With the greatest of pleasure, Ms Southwell,' he said grimly, and, drawing her to his side in such a tender embrace that her lungs popped for air, he hurried her along the winding, flower-lined path.

He steered her into the lounge of their white thatched bungalow, closed the door behind them, flicked on the wall lights then, folding his arms, regarded her.

'Now, what's going on? Aren't you well, or something?'

'Yes, but you won't be if you sign that contract.'

'Oh? And what precisely do you mean by that?'

Instead of answering him immediately, Sherry crossed the room and sat down on one of the pretty bamboo-framed sofas.

'While you were away on the phone, those two men were talking. They obviously thought that, as your tame bimbo——'

His lips twitched. 'Yes. Sorry about that.'

But he didn't look in the least sorry, so she went on with a touch of asperity, 'Even an elderly bimbo like me couldn't possibly be expected to speak a word of French. So they thought they were quite safe.'

'Safe?' Tyler came across and dropped down beside her. 'Go on. You're beginning to interest me.'

She was almost enjoying herself. 'They're in quite a hurry for you to sign that sale contract, aren't they?'

'Sure, but that's the way I like to work. The sooner I get my hands on that island, the sooner construction work can start.'

'That's just the point.' She leaned back into the cushions with a little glow of triumph. 'There won't be any construction work. The reason they want your signature now is that they're afraid the news will leak out before you've bought the island.'

'What news?'

'I couldn't get it all, I'm afraid—well, I wasn't really listening at that stage—but it's something about a rare bird that was thought to be extinct and now a pair's been found on that island. And the government is about to declare the island a protected reserve, with no building permitted.'

'*What?*'

Well, if she'd wanted to knock him sideways, she'd certainly succeeded.'

'I didn't know what to do,' she went on. 'I was going to say it right out—confront them with it—but I thought it might be better to wait till I could tell you.'

'What a very sensible young woman you are,' he said tightly, and she could almost feel the anger in him— and, more than that, his quicksilver mind clicking into action.

'I-I'm sorry about back there.' She bit her lip as she felt her cheeks turn rose-pink. 'But I had to get you away from the table somehow, and the only thing I could think of was putting on that act.'

'Oh?' He raised one dark eyebrow. 'So that's what it was—just an act. You do disappoint me.'

She coloured even more. 'Yes, of course. You know it was.' Clearing her throat, she went on determinedly, 'Anyway, what are you going to do?'

'Well, long term——' at the sight of his face, Sherry felt a little shiver run through her '—I intend to get even with those two bastards. But short term——'

He stood up, strode into his bedroom and, as Sherry strained her ears, she heard him punching out numbers on his bedside telephone.

'Ed? Hi, this is Tyler. . . Yeah. I'm on Bora Bora— got in yesterday. . . Sure. I'm aiming to look you up while I'm here. How are you and Riva?. . . Great. But now listen, Ed—this isn't exactly a social call. I need some info—and fast.'

Outside, a little breeze sprang up and Tyler's bedroom door swung to so that, even though she strained to hear even more, the rest of the one-sided conversation was lost.

Heavens, how tired she was. Her eyes were gritty, prickling with fatigue. Yawning hugely, she kicked off her high-heeled sandals and tucked her feet under her on the sofa. Unclipping her silver filigree earrings, she dropped them on to the small table beside her, did the same with the matching necklace, then finally unpinned her hair from its tightly coiled chignon, running her fingers through it with a groan of relief.

She yawned again. It looked as though Tyler's phone

call was going to take half the night, so she might as well go to bed. When she'd realised that they were sharing this bungalow, so discreetly secluded, as all the guest accommodation was, for a moment a *frisson* of that terror from the swimming-pool in Bristol had shivered through her.

But then she'd seen that they each had their own en suite rooms. And besides she hoped that, without actually spelling it out, she'd made it very plain—just in case he had any different ideas—that the only mutual meeting ground would be the sitting-room, and the veranda where they had taken breakfast together that morning.

Her bedroom, with its airy coolness, seemed very tempting now, but maybe she ought to wait and see what Tyler discovered. She settled herself more comfortably on the cushions and closed her eyes. . .

She roused to hear rapid footsteps, but before she could do more than half open her eyes she felt herself being snatched up into a pair of powerful arms and whirled around, her hair streaming behind her.

'Sherry—you're wonderful!' Tyler exclaimed jubilantly, but as she looked breathlessly up at him his smile faded and, just as abruptly, he set her down again.

The room was still reeling around her though, so that she gave a little gasp and clung to him. He lifted her up once more, but gently this time, placed her on the sofa then dropped down beside her.

'Sorry about that. Are you all right?'

'Well, just a bit dizzy, that's all.' But she didn't look at him. 'I think I must still be jet lagged.'

Though deep inside her she knew that it wasn't jet

lag which was responsible for that unnerving fluttering sensation, but rather the sensation of being held close to Tyler, so close that she'd actually felt his warm breath on her cheek, the strong beat of his heart against her ribs.

'Anyway,' she had to force herself to go on, 'did you find out anything?'

'Plenty.' He gave a mirthless laugh. 'You were quite right. That guy I rang, he's a friend from way back.' When he glanced at her she nodded quickly, not wanting him to know that she had been eavesdropping. 'He's a journalist—runs a tourist paper out here—and he says the last couple of days there's been a strong rumour that some goddamn bird—Polynesian sand-piper, or something—that's supposed to have been extinct for the last two hundred years has turned up on that island—with the specific intention, no doubt, of thwarting my plans.'

'Oh.' She looked at him, her eyes round. 'So the rest is probably true.'

'About the place being made a reserve? More than likely, Ed thinks. Some local environmental group has got on to it, and, as everybody's busy turning green these days, yours truly was nearly had for a sucker.' He gave her a rather shaken smile. 'In my hurry, I'd have landed Brennan with a highly expensive, highly useless piece of Pacific real estate—the very last thing the company can do with right now.'

He picked up her hand, almost absently it seemed, and brushed his lips across the palm. 'Thanks, Sherry.'

Their eyes met across it, and something seemed to spark between them, shiver in the air then fade, but it was enough to make her pull back her hand sharply.

'Oh, think nothing of it—all part of my very highly paid PA job,' she said lightly, but she heard the faint current of uncertainty beneath her casual tone. 'So, what do you intend doing about it?' She couldn't stop herself adding, 'Accept defeat gracefully, no doubt.'

He met her eye, then said blandly, 'Is that what I'm supposed to do—as an archetypal Gemini, that is?'

'Not exactly, no.' Remembering his face when she'd first told him of what she'd heard she went on, 'I'd expect you to do something more along the lines of making sure that those two gentlemen didn't feel like unloading any more redundant islands for quite some time.'

Tyler laughed grimly. 'Sure. But after that?'

Springing to his feet, he pulled off his jacket, tossing it across a chair, then, with a grimace, dragged off his tie and opened the top button of his white shirt.

'That's better. How I hate dressing up,' he said and began pacing up and down the polished floorboards, his hands in his pockets, a morose scowl settling on his dark features.

Sherry watched him for several minutes, knowing herself to be quite forgotten, then as fatigue oozed through her brain like a grey miasma, she began to struggle to her feet.

Tyler halted in mid-stride. 'Where are you off to?' Then, as she stood swaying gently on her feet, he gave her a rueful grin. 'Sorry, honey. Bed for you.'

Before she could draw back, he scooped her up into his arms and carried her along the wide passage to her bedroom at the rear of the bungalow. Shouldering open the door, he carried her in then very slowly set her down, letting her body trickle through his hands until her toes met firm ground.

The only light was the moonlight, filtering in through half-closed shutters. In it, Tyler's face, and most of all his eyes, had taken on a strange, silvery quality. For a few endless seconds they stared at one another, then very slowly he bent his head and she felt his lips brush across hers, to and fro, gentle, hypnotic, erotic, until all the feeling in her body seemed to have focused itself into her lips so that nothing of her existed beyond them, and they opened beneath him, parting softly.

As her eyes closed, she felt his mouth slide slowly down her throat, until it came to rest against the frantically beating pulse at the base.

'Oh, Tyler, what are you doing?' It came out as a shaky breath.

Against her skin he whispered huskily, 'I'm in the process of forgetting that I never mix business with pleasure.'

The words hit her like a douche of cold water. She jerked back sharply out of his arms, turned away and flicked a switch so that her bedside light came on, instantly breaking that fatal spell which the tropical night, the moon and Tyler Brennan were weaving in her mind.

He stared at her for a moment, then said brusquely, 'Goodnight, Sherry. Sleep well.' And without another glance he had gone.

She stood listening, her trembling hands clasped together, as he went down the passage, back to the sitting-room, and along to his bedroom. Then, drawing one shuddering breath, she roused herself, pulled off her dress and went through to the bathroom, banging the door to behind her, as though finally to rupture that spell.

She was far too exhausted to shower, but even tonight the years of self-discipline forced her to cleanse her face as carefully as ever. While she rigidly followed her nightly routine, though, she took good care to avoid any direct confrontation with her reflection, terrified of what she might see lurking in her eyes.

Finally, she splashed her face with cool water, went back to the bedroom, switched off the light and collapsed between the sheets.

But if she'd expected to tumble straight into sleep she was disappointed. The previous night, after the long flight, the bed had come up to meet her and it had been like falling into a black pit. Tonight, though, everything was different. Just the other side of that wall was Tyler. Every soft creak wasn't a little animal outside, but Tyler padding around, first in his bathroom then in the bedroom, and every soft rustle was not a tiny insect out there on the veranda but Tyler, getting undressed, maybe putting on that black silk kimono with the golden dragon curling itself around his naked body——

Sherry's eyes widened in horror. What on earth was she doing? Surely she wasn't—*couldn't be*—stupid enough to fall for another Gemini—and this man was a Gemini of Geminis.

No, of course she wasn't.

Angrily, she flung herself over on to her other side, squeezed her eyes tight shut and willed herself to sleep. Out here, though, you couldn't count sheep—woolly sheep just didn't fit on Bora Bora. Instead, she forced herself to start counting the tiny waves as they ran up the beach, creaming among the pebbles. One—two—three—four. . .

But many hundreds of waves had broken before at last, that little frown still creasing her brow, she drifted into a restless sleep.

CHAPTER FIVE

Not morning already. Sherry groaned inwardly as the brisk knocking finally dredged her out from her dream.

The door opened but she kept her head half hidden under the pillow, her eyes screwed shut—a bright, bouncy Polynesian maid, like the one who'd brought their breakfast yesterday, she just could not face this morning. She caught the delicious aroma of coffee, the clink of china, soft footsteps, and then there was silence.

Mmmm. She turned over lazily and was already drifting off again when her bare shoulder twitched under a sudden draught of warm air. Then the draught came again, curling across her skin, and this time behind it she heard a faint movement, while at the same moment her nostrils received a drift of spicy sandalwood aftershave that was surely familiar.

Instantly tense in every muscle, she turned over again—and came face to face with Tyler. He was down on his haunches beside her bed, elbows resting on the mattress, chin propped on his knuckles, lips already pursed to breathe on her again.

'Good morning, Ms Southwell.'

Through the pale darkness, she saw the gleam of white teeth. For a stunned instant she stared at him through her dishevelled hair then, as her gaze fell, she realised that she was lying sprawled across the bed, on—not under—the sheet, and stark naked.

With a gasp of horror she rolled away, simultaneously dragging the tangled sheet across her, clutching it to her like a lifebelt.

'H-how did you get in?'

'Well, I turned the door-handle and it——'

'You know what I mean,' she said, but her voice was still infuriatingly breathy.

The last time she'd seen him had been just a few minutes earlier, and the memory of that encounter was still throwing her totally off balance. Her final dream of the night—he'd taken it over completely. She'd been lying on a beach; she didn't know exactly where, but the sand was soft, the air perfumed with flowers, the sound of water in her ears—and he'd walked up to her, purposefully, like a cat, and stood looking down at her, his grey eyes glittering, then his hands had reached for her——

Horrified, Sherry realised that under the sheet her nipples were tautening at the memory of what those lean brown hands, now just inches away from her, had done to her. Dry-throated with shame, she felt a tide of scarlet crawl over her flesh. Such a dream could only be the effects of jet lag, it had to be, for if she was going to make a habit of having dreams like that she wouldn't dare close her eyes all night from now on.

'Right—time to get up. I don't employ idle little slobs.'

Tyler gave the sheet a warning tug then, when she gave a squeak of terror, uncoiled himself and went across to open the shutters, flooding the room with dazzling light which made her wince.

She half sat up, clutching the sheet to her with one hand.

'Give me my nightie, please. It's over there.' Being cocooned in a sheet gave her not the slightest sense of security, with Tyler Brennan loose in her bedroom.

He picked up the sleepshirt which, some time during the night, she had dragged off and flung away, and held it up by the shoulders, an expression of extreme distaste on his handsome features.

'What the hell are these?' He shook it slightly, so that the blue and green fishes rippled through their stylised turquoise waves.

She glared at him. 'What do you think they are? My Piscean fish, of course.'

Tyler gave a bark of laughter. 'Of course. Why did I ask? But anyway, what's happened to the silk night-dresses I bought you?'

'Oh, it—it's too hot out here for them,' she mumbled.

'Too hot?' He raised one dark brow in delicate disbelief. 'Silk, my dear Sherry, is the only thing— apart from her own delectable skin, that is——' his voice seemed to wrap itself around her, and as their eyes met she found herself quite unable to tear hers away '—in which a woman feels she is wearing nothing at all.'

He was doing it again, weaving a spell around her with only his voice as a weapon.

'You know something?' she said belligerently. 'I think you've got some sort of fetish about silk.'

But he only gave her a slow smile. 'Hasn't every man?'

'I don't know,' she said crossly. 'Probably, knowing men.' She snatched at the nightshirt as he tossed it at her. 'Now, go away.'

'Certainly not. I want to talk to you.' And very deliberately he sat down on the bed, so that she was forced to wriggle into the shirt under cover of the sheet.

When she emerged, tousle-haired, she allowed herself to look at him properly for the first time that morning. He was wearing white canvas shorts and a navy T-shirt, the outfit's very casualness somehow enhancing that impression he always gave of indolent grace, side by side with intense masculinity.

Sherry eyed him resentfully. It just wasn't fair—he really did thrive on a handful of hours of sleep. She was still bleary-eyed and more than a touch edgy, and here he was, fresh, relaxed, as usual, sleek and glossy as a panther—and about as lethal.

She sat forward, hugging her knees. 'Have you done anything about that island yet?'

'Well,' he grimaced, 'I spent half the night wondering where I could hire a Smith and Wesson——'

'A *gun*, you mean?' Sherry almost shrieked the word, then she clutched his arm. 'Oh, no, Tyler, *please*—you mustn't. Those men——'

'Oh, no, not them. Those damn birds—just two quick shots would solve everything. Although maybe,' he added reflectively, 'now you mention it, I just might have a go at those two bastards as well. Only joking, Sherry.' He grinned as her eyes dilated with horror.

'Are you sure?' she asked doubtfully.

'Quite sure.' And before she could draw back he leaned forward and trailed his little finger in a soft, butterfly gesture across her full lower lip. 'After all, I wouldn't want to be hauled off to gaol just now.' His voice dropped a fraction to a seductive caress. 'I have much more important things in mind.'

'You mean, finding another island?' Somehow she managed to meet his eyes full-on this time.

'Well, yes, that as well,' he said smoothly, and again, fleetingly, the expression in his eyes as they rested on her made every pulse skitter with nervous unease.

She cleared her throat. 'What are we doing today? Are we going into Vaitape?'

He grinned, showing those perfect white teeth again. 'I've already been. I looked in on you,' her eyes met his once more then slid away hastily, 'to see if you wanted to come, but you were dead to the world. But that reminds me. Close your eyes.'

'I most certainly——'

'Be quiet and do as you're told.' He scowled at her. 'You know, Ms Southwell, excellent PA as I knew you'd turn out to be, you really must learn one more lesson if you want to be perfect.'

She eyed him warily. 'What's that?'

'I like my women submissive—obedient to my every whim.'

I bet you do, she thought. Aloud, 'But I'm not your woman. I'm your PA—for two years. Remember?'

He shrugged. 'Is there a difference? Now, close your eyes.'

Sherry did. Every sense on watch, she heard a rustle, then something soft dropped into her lap.

'OK—open them.'

When she did so, a large, silver-wrapped parcel lay across her knees.

'Undo it, then.'

Tyler sat back, grinning, as her fingers went hesitantly to the first knot. She pulled the tissue apart, then lifted out——

'Oh,' she breathed. The fragile silk lay in a blue-green mound, and when she lifted it it hung from her hands like a weightless cloud, the fine gold thread which ran through it gleaming dully.

'Indulging my silk fetish again, I'm afraid.' He smiled at her unrepentantly. 'But at least it's your colour, isn't it? Sea-green for Ms Pisces, I mean.'

He'd taken the trouble to choose the one colour which she loved above all others. Quite unable to trust her voice, she nodded.

'So you like it?'

'It's beautiful.'

She gazed at him across the drift of silk, her brown eyes huge.

'Well, every girl needs a *pareu* in Polynesia.'

Sherry bit her lip in embarrassment. 'But you've bought me so much already. I can't possibly accept it.'

'Of course you can,' he replied brusquely. 'It's a small thank-you for last night, saving my face—and a hell of a lot of Brennan money. Now, get dressed.'

Her eyes went to the wardrobe, where a row of clothes hung. 'Shall I wear one of those linen dresses?'

'Certainly not.' The expensive outfits were dismissed with a peremptory gesture. 'Wear that.' He jerked his thumb at the *pareu*.

'But——'

'That'll be perfect, with your bikini. No work today—we're playing hookey.'

'But I thought——'

'Sssh.' He laid a long finger against her lips. 'You

know something, Ms Southwell? You think far too much. Now——' he glanced at his watch '—five minutes.'

'But I haven't had my breakfast yet.'

He paused, one hand on the door. 'Six, then.' And he had gone.

Sherry expelled a long breath. She'd known, when she took on this job, that life with Tyler would be life spent permanently in the fast track. But even so——

Leaping out of bed, she padded over to the table where he had placed her tray. A bowl of tropical fruit, freshly squeezed orange juice, a plate of croissants and brioches, a pot of fragrant coffee. A breakfast to linger over, savouring every delicious mouthful. Ah, well. She shrugged philosophically, poured a cup of coffee, gulped it down, tore off a piece of warm, feathery brioche and crammed it into her mouth, then went through to the bathroom. . .

She was still struggling with the *pareu* when behind her the bedroom door opened.

'Ready?' Then, 'No, not like that.' Tyler sounded pained. 'You look like a sack of potatoes.'

'Maybe that's what I want to look like,' she retorted, but her voice sounded fluttery again, for his hands had already thrust hers aside. Peeling the *pareu* away from where she had tucked it inelegantly but securely under her armpits, carefully covering her bikini top, he let it slowly drop, his fingers brushing against her skin until it rested on the curve of her hips, just below her navel and above the line of her bikini pants.

'Those girls were showing us all how to wear them, before dinner last night. Weren't you watching?'

He was frowning, all his attention on getting the perfect hang of the silk.

'Well, you certainly were,' she said maliciously.

He raised his eyes and gave her a smug, panther's smile. 'Jealous?'

'Certainly not.'

But all the same it had been an unpleasant little sensation which had jarred through her body, as she'd watched his open enjoyment of the curvaceous, brown-eyed girl standing in front of him, hips swaying gently as she expertly manipulated her flowered *pareu*.

'Of course not,' she repeated, more loudly, and backed away from his hands.

There was a full-length mirror on the wall. She turned to it, then gave a little involuntary gasp as she saw herself. Her bikini, though a pretty turquoise, was perfectly ordinary. But the silk *pareu* had subtly transformed her, so that she too had become a lissom, swaying, yielding nymph.

Her eyes enormous, her soft lips parted, she stared at herself, not at all sure that she liked this new creature, then turned away abruptly, putting her hands to her sun-streaked hair to draw it into a knot.

'Leave it,' Tyler's voice commanded.

'But I prefer to wear it up.'

'And I prefer you wear it down.'

She made a move to catch it up, their eyes met, and she dropped her hands. After all, it was safer to let him win these little bouts—that way, he'd think he'd won the war. Although quite what war was being waged—and what its spoils would be—she preferred not to ask herself.

* * * *

'Come and steer.'

Sherry hesitated. For the past half-hour she had been perfectly happy to sit watching Tyler's back as he stood at the controls of the powerful motor boat, his legs slightly apart, his bare feet gripping the deck against the roll of the waves. But then, as he beckoned, she got up obediently and went forward.

He pulled her in front of him and she put her hands on the wheel, within his, then stood encircled lightly by his arms, feeling the skin on his forearms brush softly against the hairs on hers so that they prickled and stood on end.

She made herself stand rigid, with the only points of contact of their two bodies the brush of arm against arm or fingertips meeting as the wheel swung. But then a series of sharp little waves slapping against the hull caught her off balance and she stumbled back, fetching up against his hard body.

With a mumbled apology, she went to move away but he closed in behind her, trapping her against the wheel.

'Carry on. You're doing fine.'

His voice softly soothed her and gradually, intoxicated by the wind, the sea, the thrum of the powerful motor, she let herself relax into the pleasure of the moment.

'Where are we going—Bali H'ai?' She looked round at him, and he laughed.

'Oh, sure. And we'll have Bloody Mary waiting on the beach for us. No—see that?' He leaned across her shoulder so that his warm breath stirred the tendrils on the back of her neck and jabbed a finger at a faint blue smudge on the horizon. 'That's the *motu* we're heading for.'

He spun the wheel in a half-turn and the wind caught at her long, caramel-coloured hair, whipping it across his face.

'Oh, sorry, Cap'n.' She gave him a mock salute.

'Watch it, young lady.' He growled threateningly. 'We're in *Mutiny on the Bounty* country here, you know. Any more of that, and it'll be walking-the-plank time for you.'

'Oh, not that, sir!' she squealed in mock terror. 'Anything but that, sir.'

'Anything?'

He raised one sardonic eyebrow then made a grab at her but, giggling, she wriggled out of his grasp and he had to snatch at the wheel instead, leaving her free to tuck the silky strands firmly back behind her ears.

Long minutes later, though, as she gripped on the wheel again, her heart was still thumping erratically. What on earth was happening to her? She'd never laughed like this, in such joyous freedom, with Mike— or any other man.

Mike! The name jolted her sharply. She hadn't given a thought—not one single, fleeting thought—to Mike for over a week. Of course, he'd treated her abominably, but even so. . . A twinge of guilt shot through her. Just eight days ago she'd really believed she loved him. How could she have been so fickle? A rueful grimace flickered across her face. Well, at least she knew now the sure-fire cure for a broken heart. A week with Tyler Kavanagh Brennan—but only, of course, she amended hastily, because out in the fast lane with him your feet didn't touch the ground.

That pale blue smudge was turning rapidly into a small island, with a low craggy hill at the centre, lapped by a green tide of palms stretching down to a fringe of white sand. Just ahead of them was a line of jagged rocks where the surf was breaking, and one narrow gap like a broken tooth in a mouth.

'Hold tight,' Tyler shouted, then, before she had time to be frightened, he ran the boat in through the space in the boiling waves and into calm water.

'Not scared, were you?' He grinned down at her, his grey eyes dancing with exhilaration. 'Don't worry, Sherry—you're perfectly safe with me.'

And she was still trying to work out whether he meant on the sea or something else entirely when he began skilfully manoeuvring in alongside a dilapidated jetty. He hoisted out the picnic box that he'd stowed away back at the hotel, then leaping lithely ashore turned and, putting out his hand, swung her up beside him.

The sand was fine and as white as icing sugar. Sherry kicked off her sandals and followed him up the beach, revelling in the softness under her toes, then watched as he set down the cool-box in the shade of an overhanging frangipani tree. He took out a bottle of white wine and wedged it securely between two stones in the little stream which bubbled out from a tangle of lilac bougainvillaea further in among the trees.

And all the time she watched him with that same half-fearful, half-excited knotting of her stomach, quite unable to tear her eyes from his lean, muscled frame, the thatch of black hair, slightly over-long and curling into his neck in little drake's tails.

Finally, he scooped up a handful of water and

cautiously sipped it. 'Mmmm—great. Come and taste it.'

Reluctantly, she went over to him, hitching up her *pareu* as she went down on her haunches beside him. Before she could lean forward, though, he lifted another scoop of water between both hands and held it for her. Obediently, with every fibre of her body tingling with the awareness of him, she sipped the ice-cold water as it trickled through his fingers and fell on the soft ground like diamonds. Or like tears——

Abruptly, Sherry leapt to her feet and blundered back to the beach. After a few yards, he caught her up, his face bland, as though he had noticed nothing of her inner turmoil. Casually draping an arm across her shoulders, he pulled her to him as they walked. . .

They had encircled the tiny island, pushed through the tangled scrub of undergrowth to the foot of the hill, climbed to its summit, stood on the beach watching a school of flying fish skim to and fro, and finally come back to the frangipani tree.

Dropping on to his knees, Tyler unclipped the cool-box and began piling food—pâté, salad, cold marinated fish, bread rolls—on to two plates. He cut a lemon in half, deftly twisted it, sprinkling juice over the fish, then handed her a plate.

'Thanks.'

But she did not look at him. In fact, she hadn't been able to meet his eye since that moment when she'd turned from watching the flying fish, her face glowing, and seen that he was watching not the fish but her. The expression in his grey eyes had been one which had made her lungs tighten, as if the air were being squeezed out of them, and forced her heart to skip a beat—and another—and another, before finally she could drag her eyes away and, very pale beneath her tan, rivet her gaze on those leaping fish. . .

'More wine?' Tyler broke a silence that had lasted a long time.

'Yes, please.'

Sherry held out her glass, thinking as she watched him fill it with pale gold liquid that she really shouldn't—she never had more than two glasses. Today, though, was so hot, and that delicious fish had been so highly seasoned.

She took a sip then, in an effort to break the constraint which seemed to have settled on them both, said brightly, 'This place is paradise. You know, it would be perfect for your new hotel.'

'You think so?' Absently, he was tracing a pattern in the sand with his forefinger.

'Oh, yes. You'd want to keep everything at a low level, of course, not to spoil it, but you could have bungalows spread out over there among those palm trees.'

'Really?'

'Yes. And the dining area could be——' her eyes ranged over the scene before her '—right here, built on stilts over the sand.' She was getting quite carried away with enthusiasm, but he shook his head firmly.

'Uh-uh. I've already decided that's going over there.' He pointed to the headland at one end of the lagoon. 'The sun sets that way, so the guests will have a superb free floorshow while they have dinner.'

She stared at him. 'You've decided? You mean

you've already made up your mind?' And when he nodded, 'But how do you know that this island's for sale?'

'A few phone calls this morning—while you were still getting your beauty sleep.'

'Oh.' She was feeling rather deflated.

'I checked out what was on the market—and this time made sure there were no goddamn sandpipers lurking in the undergrowth. And now I've seen it I'm buying it.'

She laughed shakily. 'Tell me, do you *always* move this fast?'

He gave her a long look. 'When I want something badly enough, yes, I move very fast indeed.'

Sherry looked away, tucking her hair behind her ears in a nervous gesture. 'Er—so we aren't playing hookey today?'

'Not entirely, no—I never do.'

'And all morning, when I thought we were just looking around, you've been working.'

He raised his brows. 'Not criticising your employer's work technique, I trust?' There was a touch of acidity in his tone.

'Oh, no, not at all,' she said hastily. 'I was just——'

'Good. Because you know what they say. All work and no play makes Tyler a very dull boy.'

Leaning forward, he delved in the cool-box and reached out some fruit.

'Oh, gorgeous. I didn't know peaches grew here.' She took one and softly stroked the velvety skin.

'I'm not sure that they do. These were flown in from the States, I think. No,' as she went to take a bite, 'there's only one way to eat a peach. Here, let me show you.'

He took it from her and split it, the golden juice trickling over his fingers, cut out the stone then laid the two halves on a plate and poured wine from his glass into each cavity.

'Now, try that. No, not a spoon—just your tongue.'

And he held up the plate, so that Sherry, rather self-consciously at first, could lap the peach juice which, mingled with the wine, made a honey-sweet scented nectar that made her senses reel.

Above her bent head she heard Tyler give a soft chuckle. 'You know something? You look exactly like a kitten—that little pink tongue going in and out, so—uh—sexy.'

Sherry's tongue stilled. She looked up at him, her eyes darkening.

'Don't—please don't, Tyler,' she whispered huskily. 'You know I don't like it—don't want it.'

He gave her a lazy smile. 'I know you *think* you don't like it, Sherry. But that's a very different thing. And as for wanting——'

'*No.*' She drew back sharply, snatching the plate from him. 'I'll finish the rest with a spoon,' she said stiffly, and turned away.

Of course, he wanted her. She knew that—had known it right from the very beginning, but she'd stubbornly refused to acknowledge the fact. And what Tyler Brennan wanted he had to have—she also knew that. Yet surely, if she so chose, she would be safe. He was not the sort of man to force himself on her—so, yes, she was perfectly safe.

Just now, he was sprawled almost full length, his

glass of wine balanced on his stomach, one arm resting negligently across his thigh, the hand open in total relaxation. Sherry found her eyes drawn to that inner wrist, where the skin was finer, paler than the rest of his arm. Just beneath the surface she could see the blue vein, and beside it she saw the movement of the skin where the pulse was beating.

She stared down as though mesmerised by that pulse until dimly she realised that her own pulse had taken the same time and was beating in unison. Everything else had receded from her and all she could hear were those two pulses thundering in her ears, as the blood in her veins coagulated to a slow, honeyed thickness. It was as though their two bodies were joined, the rhythm they shared building and building to a shattering climax——

She sensed Tyler begin to turn his head towards her and jerked hers away, but not before the betraying colour had flared in her cheeks. She closed her eyes and tried to take deep, calming breaths. It's only the wine, she told herself fiercely. That's what's making me like this. The wine, the sun, the surf beating on this glorious, unbelievable shore—and nothing, absolutely nothing else.

CHAPTER SIX

SHERRY sat motionless for a long time, her head still turned away. But then she gave a start as something dropped on to her bare stomach in a featherlight caress. Jerking round, she saw that it was a flower from one of the nearby bougainvillaea bushes.

It trembled on her midriff like a purple butterfly, but before she could brush it away a suntanned hand snaked out, took it and began idly flicking it back and forth against the other hand. Flick. . .flick. . . In the oppressive afternoon heat, the silence weighed heavy between them.

'I. . .' She cleared her throat nervously and began again. 'I always think bougainvillaea is a really ugly name for a lovely flower.'

'I'm sure Louis Antoine wouldn't be pleased to hear you say that.'

'Who?'

'Louis Antoine de Bougainville, of course. He was one of the first Europeans to come this way, and the plant's named after him.'

'Oh, I didn't know that.' They seemed, by common consent, to have edged on to safer ground, and she was able to look at him enquiringly.

He grinned. 'Actually, I didn't, either, till I read it in the guidebook. Over my leisurely breakfast this morning,' he added meaningfully.

'Yes, well, just because you only need three hours' sleep a night.'

'Life's too short to waste on sleeping.' He flashed her another grin. 'And you also don't know, I imagine, about his female crew member.'

'Female?'

'Yes. One of his officers smuggled her on board disguised as a man, and she made it from France to Tahiti with no one—apart, that is, from the lucky officer—any the wiser.'

Without warning, he reached across and gently brushed the floweret across her midriff, circling the navel then back.

'Of course,' his voice had dropped to a throaty purr, 'some women could never get away with that sort of thing.'

'You think so?' But Sherry could not match his easy tone.

'I know so.' His gaze travelled lazily up to the soft feminine curves of her breasts, and she felt her flesh quiver and tingle as though his eyes were touching her, like soft probing fingers.

She tried to protest but her tongue was sticking to the roof of her mouth. She wanted to leap to her feet and run away, but instead she felt herself losing all power over her limbs, drowning in a sea of lush, perfumed sensuality.

'*No.*' It came out as a despairing whimper, but then, as she saw momentarily the spark of triumph in his grey eyes, it gave her just enough strength to save herself.

She jerked upright, snapping the spell. 'I've told you—don't.'

'Don't what?'

'You know perfectly well—trying to s-seduce me.'

He gave her a look of wounded innocence. 'But, Sherry, I haven't laid a finger on you.'

'I know you haven't, damn you—you don't have to.' She heard herself saying the appalling words, and broke off with a little gasp of shock, but not before she had seen him give that little secret panther's smile. Through her fear came a spurt of ice-cold anger. 'I thought you told me, when I took this job, that you didn't agree with mixing business with pleasure.'

Tyler's hand swept in an indolent curve, encompassing the snow-white beach, the aquamarine sea, the palms swaying softly overhead. 'You call this business?'

'Well, what about the other rule of the house—no sexual liaisons between Brennan employees?'

'But you see, Sherry,' he drawled, 'I'm not a Brennan employee—I'm a Brennan.'

'And in your twisted view I suppose that makes all the difference,' she snapped.

He spread his hands. 'But of course.'

But his lazy arrogance only stiffened her resolve to hold him off. 'You're wasting your time, Tyler. You see, apart from anything else, I don't trust you.'

His dark brows came down in a scowl. 'Why the hell not?'

'Because—because you're a Gemini, that's why.'

'Not that again!' He shook his head in angry disbelief. 'And just what has that got to do with it, anyway?'

'Everything,' she said coldly. 'You Geminis—you're all lying, worthless two-timers.'

Her lips gave a bitter twist on the final words, and his eyes narrowed.

'You really think that, don't you?' When she

nodded, he went on slowly, 'Just by any chance, Sherry—was Lloyd a Gemini?'

'Mike? However did you guess?' She gave a brief, humourless laugh.

'But you can't judge us all by that swine, you know.' A new gentleness had entered his voice, which for a moment made her want to weep, but then cynicism took over again. This was all part of the Gemini technique, wasn't it—as she knew all too well?

'Really?' she retorted. 'Sorry, but, you see, I know better.'

'But you only knew Lloyd a month, didn't you?'

'Yes, well,' she made a feeble attempt at an insouciant shrug, 'perhaps he wasn't the first Gemini I've had experience of.'

'Tell me, Sherry.' Before she could draw back out of reach, he took her hand, holding it firmly.

'No, I don't want to talk about it.'

'Oh, yes, you do.'

She rounded on him, eyes blazing. 'Why the hell do you always think you know better than I what I want?'

'Maybe because I do.'

When she tried to snatch her hand free, he held on to it and began stroking his thumb back and forth across her palm until gradually the tension inside her began to ease.

'Come on, Sherry, tell me.'

'All right.' She gave him a lop-sided smile. 'One pathetic little story coming up. I met Piers when I went to work for him—he was an estate agent in Dover. We became engaged.' Her voice, hesitant at first, was becoming jerky as she speeded up. 'I-I moved in with him. We talked about marriage—at least, when I thought about it afterwards, *I* did, but he always seemed to have a million good reasons for putting it off.'

She stared down at his thumb, still circling her palm, but hardly seeing it. 'And then he opened an office in Normandy, to cash in on English people wanting to buy properties in northern France. My French is good——'

'I know that,' he put in softly.

'—and to Piers, at least, it seemed a great idea for me to spend more and more of my time over there. Of course, I didn't guess—not for a long time—what he was getting up to, with twenty miles of English Channel safely between us. I found out in the end, but he persuaded me to forgive him.'

'And you did, of course.'

'Of course.' She laughed bitterly. 'If he was a classic Gemini, well, I was the perfect Piscean—the ever-loving, all-forgiving victim, ready and willing to be trampled all over.'

'Well,' he said slowly, 'perhaps just one peccadillo——'

'One! And two, and three and four. But even when I knew, I still hung on for months. In the end, though, I-I. . .' she bent her head so that her hair swung forward, screening her hot face '. . .refused to sleep with him—I couldn't bear to—and we broke up. I moved to Bristol to make a fresh start, and met Mike. End of story.'

There was silence for a moment, then Tyler said softly, 'Of course, not making any excuses for that bastard Piers, but marriage just isn't for everybody, you know.'

She raised her brown eyes and studied him intently. 'That sounds like personal experience.'

'You could say that,' he grunted.

'But I thought you hadn't been married.' For some reason, the thought of Tyler married, even in the distant past, gave her that disturbing, vaguely unpleasant little feeling again.

'No more I have. But I witnessed at first hand my parents fighting their war of attrition for years, before my mother finally walked out.'

Instinctively, she put her hand over his. 'I'm sorry.'

He shrugged. 'It was a long time ago. Although, of course, since then I've had the example of my two elder brothers—just to drive the message home.'

'So marriage isn't for you?' She didn't know whether she was glad or sorry when he gave a disparaging laugh.

'Too right it isn't.' His eyes dropped to her slim hand as it rested on his. 'Your ex-fiancé—did he, by any chance, give you that?'

'What?'

'That bracelet.'

She glanced down and saw the fine silver chain bracelet, with the half-dozen tiny turquoise-eyed fishes dangling from it.

'Yes.' She raised her arm to study it then went on slowly, 'He wanted me to get rid of Albert Edward——'

'Albert Edward?' Tyler looked astonished.

'My old teddy-bear. Piers said it was babyish to hang on to him.' She gave a faint smile. 'I think he was almost jealous—I was very fond of Albert.'

'And did you?' He sounded angry.

'Oh, yes, of course. Well,' this time the smile was

half ashamed, 'I never could stand up to him. Anyway, when I did, he bought me this bracelet.'

'For being a good, dutiful little girl, I suppose,' he said grimly. 'Throw it away.'

She gaped at him. 'What?'

'Throw it away,' he repeated imperiously. 'I won't have you keeping anything of that swine's.'

Sherry jutted her chin. 'Now, look here—just because you've wheedled all these pitiful little stories out of me, that doesn't mean you own me body and soul. Oh——'

An outraged gasp was torn from her as Tyler leaned forward, caught hold of the bracelet with both hands, ripped open the clasp and sent it spinning in a glittering arc into the sea.

Springing to her feet, she glared down at him. 'How dare you? Do you know something? You really are an overbearing, arrogant bully.'

'Now you don't really think that, Sherry. And anyway, you know it's for your own good.'

No, she didn't. The fact that that very morning she'd looked at the bracelet, wondering whether to give it to the maid when she left Bora Bora, had no bearing on things whatsoever.

'There you go again,' she stormed. 'Telling me what's good for me.' She pointed a dramatic finger down the beach. 'Come and help me look for it.'

Very leisurely, Tyler got to his feet and brushed the sand off his elegant frame, then began walking along the beach.

'Where are you going?'

'Back to work,' he said over his shoulder. 'Coming?'

'No, I'm going to look for my bracelet,' she shouted after him.

He stopped and turned. 'You do that—but if you do you're an even bigger fool than I took you for.' And he swung on his heel and strode off.

Sherry, nursing her tingling wrist, stood glowering at his back, but then as he turned in among the palm trees she pulled off her *pareu*, flung it in a heap and went off down the beach, her feet scuffing up the sand in furious little spurts.

Wading into the water, she walked slowly up and down, head lowered, until at last, incredulously, her eyes lighted on a pale glimmer, half hidden by the drifting sand. With a cry of triumph she bent and brought up the bracelet.

It was undamaged, apart from the clasp which Tyler had wrenched, and that would be quite easy to repair. . . She looked down at it as it lay curled in her palm, then, in a slow deliberate gesture, raised her hand up above her head as though she was making an offering to the old gods of Tahiti, whose carved images she'd glimpsed among the flowered shrines on the outskirts of the villages they'd driven through. Then she drew back her hand and hurled the bracelet far out to sea.

Finally, so that she did not have to think about what she had done—or why—she plunged headlong into the translucent water and swam frantically up and down until she was gasping for breath, then went back up the beach and flopped down under the frangipani tree.

But even now she shifted and fidgeted, quite unable to settle, until at last she sat up and hunched forward, her arms clasped across her knees, lost in disturbing thought. Barely aware of what she was doing, she picked up a broken piece of shell and began making intricate, soothing patterns in the sand, until gradually the lines and curlicues turned into a recognisable shape—a stylised representation of the Gemini star sign, the twin forms interlocked, and woven within them the letters S and T.

Horrified, she stared down at what she had drawn. Then, next instant, she hurled the shell away and fiercely scrubbed the sand clean with the side of her hand. But the damage was done—those fatal letters still blazed in her brain.

Sherry gave a shuddering sigh. If she wasn't very, very careful, in spite of all her efforts she was going to allow herself to become involved with Tyler. And it wouldn't be at all like those other times. With sudden clarity, she knew that after Mike—and even after Piers—it had been mainly her wounded pride which had been so hurt. However much she'd suffered then, her heart had been dented only a very little.

But with Tyler it would be different. She wouldn't be able to walk away from him when it ended—as it was bound to. Her heart would shatter into pieces so tiny that she would spend the rest of her life trying to glue them back together again.

So, however he might feel about it, she was going to keep their relationship strictly on a working basis. Working! Good grief. Somewhere on the island, in this broiling afternoon heat, Tyler was hard at work. And she was supposed to be his PA, wasn't she, working alongside him? Perhaps that was the real reason why she'd been so fidgety—it was only guilt, after all, that while she'd been swimming and lounging here in the shade he was flogging himself to reconnoitre more of his island.

With a surge of relief, she sprang to her feet and began following that line of determined-looking footprints along the beach until they turned inland. She thrust her way through a tangle of hibiscus bushes, rampant with scarlet flowers into which tiny iridescent birds were plunging themselves in ecstasy. Standing still, she called, 'Tyler, where are you?' then, when there was no reply, pushed on further through the undergrowth.

After a few minutes she stopped again, mopping her brow, and heard very faintly the sound of running water—the same stream, perhaps, in which he had chilled the wine. She turned towards it and struggled on, the noise getting louder all the time until it was a muted thunder.

Ahead of her was a cascade of bougainvillaea, which had climbed up into the branches of a gnarled old tree and was now pouring itself back to ground level in a pink fountain. When Sherry parted the dense foliage her eyes widened in astonishment.

Just the other side of that delicate screen was a small clearing, at the far side of which the ground rose steeply. From this higher level, the stream flowed over a lip of rock to fall in a sheet of shining water among glistening ferns and mosses and on into a deep pool.

'Oh.' Sherry drew in a long breath at the beautiful scene.

But still there was no sign of Tyler. Reluctantly, she half turned to go back the way she had come, then stopped dead. He *was* there. All the time, he had been

standing motionless beside the fall, hidden from her by
the dense shade of a massive tree.

Now, though, he moved forward, the sunlight glinting on his dark head, where spray had landed. As
Sherry watched, he stood staring into the pool, then,
as though on impulse, he peeled off his T-shirt, revealing his tanned, superbly muscled torso, tossing it down
on to the mossy ground. Then his hands went to the
zip of his canvas shorts.

Sherry, all breathing suspended, her blood pounding
in her veins, stood absolutely motionless. That satin-
smooth skin, the play of muscles just beneath it, the
way his broad chest tapered to a slim waist, the long
curve of hip and haunch——

Tyler stepped out of his shorts, dropping them on
top of his shirt, and he was wearing now only the
briefest of black silk briefs. He was a statue, smooth as
teak and as beautiful in the shaft of sunlight which
illuminated him. And all at once it seemed as if that
same shaft lit up the dark corners of Sherry's mind.

She could no longer pretend to herself or fight
against the truth, which all day she'd battled to deny.
That morning's sensual dream, caught between sleeping and waking, had been her conscious self letting
down her guard, her subconscious struggling to make
her see reality. And now finally she did.

She wanted Tyler, as she'd never wanted any other
man. Mike and Piers had both been good-looking virile
men, but they paled into insignificance beside the aura
of sexuality that Tyler exuded, as unselfconsciously as
a magnificent wild animal. Despairingly, she felt her
whole body ache—no, hunger for him, as a starving
man craved food.

Caught in the grip of the desire—and the fear—which racked her, she moved convulsively. Above the rush of water, Tyler could not possibly have seen or heard her, but some sixth sense must have warned him, for he turned his head sharply in her direction. She saw his lips form the word 'Sherry?' then, as he took a step towards her, she jerked round to blunder blindly back through the tangled undergrowth.

Next moment, though, one bare foot caught in a protruding tree root and she fell headlong. Totally winded, she sprawled face down, until she heard footsteps and, raising herself shakily on one elbow, saw Tyler. It was her dream—he was coming towards her, purposeful, menacing.

She wanted to leap to her feet and run away again, but something stronger than herself held her prisoner so that she could only lie watching as, still clad only in the black briefs, he came slowly up to stand over her. He was blotting out the sun, so that she could not see his face.

'Sherry, why did you run away?' he asked softly.

'I——' Nervously, she ran the tip of her tongue round her lips, but her mouth was like ashes—the words would not come out.

'Sherry?' It was another question.

Wide-eyed, she gazed up at him, still quite unable to reply. The tension hissed softly in the air between them, like a snake, but then she heard him give a little sigh, as though somehow she had given him his answer.

Slowly, he came down on his knees beside her. Putting his hands under her shoulders, he lifted her into his arms and, melting into her dream, she surrendered helplessly to him.

When, still slowly, he bent his head and kissed her, her lips opened eagerly for him. His tongue probed the sweetness of her mouth, making tiny delicate thrusts at her tongue, until it tensed, quivering with delight.

As she gave a choked murmur, her eyes closed and she reached up to him to put her arms round him, her hands sliding across the sun-warmed skin of his back to draw him to her.

When he shifted his grip, she murmured in protest, but he shushed her, his mouth against hers, before pulling slightly away. She felt him release the clasp of her bikini top and drag it free, then heard his breath catch in his throat.

'Oh, Sherry, you're so beautiful.'

He cupped one breast, kneading it gently, and she felt its rosy centre pucker and harden, the nipple jutting against his palm so that she could feel the slick of sweat on it. When he lowered his mouth and took the nipple between his teeth, teasing at it, she shuddered as a pleasure so intense that it was almost pain took hold of her, and had to bite her lip to stop herself crying out.

Lifting her body to him, he trailed his mouth down it, pausing at her navel to trace erotic spirals on her trembling flesh, then on down. He ran one finger along the top of her bikini briefs, so slowly that skin dragged against skin, then, in a movement which sent every nerve-ending in her body clamouring, slid his hand inside, down over her belly until his fingers rested tantalisingly against the throbbing, pulsating centre of her.

She opened her eyes, turning her head wildly from side to side. Above her she saw the bougainvillaea screen and from behind it she heard the thunder of the cascade as it leapt and plunged into the pool.

With a little moan, she set her teeth hard on the inside of her mouth. Tyler was stirring her to the depths of her being, depths no man had ever reached before. She was utterly helpless in his arms, and he was drawing responses from her that she hadn't known she possessed, had never wanted to give. Deliberately, skilfully, mind, body and soul, he was seducing her——

Seducing!

Her eyes, blank with horror, flew open on the word. She stared down at that dark head lying across her stomach, those suntanned, skilful hands roving over her yielding flesh, just as they had done in that insidious dream. For one treacherous second she took aching, sensual pleasure in the sight. Then——

'Let me go.'

It came out as a choking, barely audible plea, but Tyler raised his head and looked at her. The expression in his eyes, dark with passion, would have filled her moments before with an elated exultation. Now, it made her rigid with terror.

'Don't touch me.'

The words burst from her and he stared at her, his grey eyes blank, his cheekbones flushed dusky red, as she huddled away from him into herself.

'Don't touch me,' she repeated. 'I-I don't want it.'

But his hands closed on her, the nails digging into her flesh as he pulled her to him. Terror flared in her. He couldn't be going to rape her—but all the same a stifled whimper was wrenched from her.

For a moment, he held her so that she sagged

helplessly in his arms. Then, his breathing ragged, his mouth twisted into a thin line—the panther deprived of his lawful prey—he said, 'Lady, for someone who *doesn't want it*,' he mimicked her voice mercilessly, 'you took one hell of a time to make up your mind.'

With a contemptuous gesture, he loosed her and Sherry, shaking in every limb as though from a high fever, rolled away from him, her arms to her naked breasts. But his cruel jibe had done one thing—it had transformed her fear into blazing anger.

'H-how dare you?'

'Oh, I dare, lady, I dare.' After that one flash of savage fury, he seemed to have himself completely under control again. 'Just one word of warning. If you make a habit of playing come-on games like that, you'll find yourself in real trouble one of these days.'

The injustice of his words flicked her like a whiplash. 'That's not fair—and you know it,' she retorted. 'Or if you don't, you ought to. I've been fighting you off all day, but you're just so—so arrogant, you can't believe that I mean it when I say no.'

'Are you quite sure that you do, Sherry?' he replied silkily.

Her hands closed until the nails bit into the palms. 'Yes, I am, damn you. I don't want to be involved with you—I don't want you.'

'Oh, but I think you do. Your mind may be saying no, but it's your body that I want—and your body is saying yes.'

'That's not true—I swear it,' she whispered.

'You're lying—at least, you're trying to. But your body can't lie.'

As she stared at him like a helpless mesmerised bird,

he raised one hand, almost casually, thrust her protective arms aside and brushed the palm softly across her breast. An involuntary gasp was dragged from her as her teacherous body responded instantly to his touch, and when she looked up through her screen of hair she saw him give a small, humourless smile.

'But I don't even like you,' she cried despairingly.

He shook his head in mock sorrow. 'My poor Sherry, what has liking ever had to do with making love?'

He was so sure of himself, so full of masculine conceit. 'Everything—in my case,' she flung back at him. 'I don't like you—let alone *love* you—so I have no intention of making love with you. Ever,' she added fiercely.

Tyler muttered something under his breath, then, putting his hands under her armpits, dragged her up into a sitting position. They faced each other, glowering.

'Look.' He was obviously reining himself in with a tremendous effort. 'You don't trust me—simply because I'm a Gemini. Yes,' he went on as she tried to interrupt. 'Oh, you can wrap it up in all sorts of sugary jargon about liking and loving, but that's it. You've had a bad time with two Gemini men. I'm another, so, in your twisted female brain—or what passes for one— you've written me off as just another untrustworthy Gemini swine.'

'That's ridiculous,' she retorted angrily. 'I'm not that stupid.'

'Aren't you? You're the one who's gone on and on *ad nauseam* about Geminis ever since we met. But just tell me this—are you going to spend the rest of your life cowering away in a cave every time a man who just happens to have been unfortunate enough to be conceived in early fall walks past?'

'If that's the way I want to run my life—yes.' She tossed back her long hair defiantly.

'So—merely through an accident of birth, we're to deprive ourselves of the pleasure of each other's bodies?'

'That's right,' she said tightly. 'And the sooner you can accept that the better it'll be for both of us.'

They stared into each other's faces, hers defiant, his closed as a fist, then, with another muttered oath, he sprang to his feet.

'Right.' His voice was like the breeze off an iceberg, and in spite of the late afternoon heat she shivered. 'Let's get back.'

Dusk was falling as they neared the hotel landing stage. Tyler cut the engine and they drifted in to bump very gently against the timbers, as Sherry sat motionless, a great sadness dragging at her heart.

The entire journey had passed in silence—not once had he turned his head to look at her, smile at her, call her over to help him steer.

Now, for the first time, he did turn towards her, and she got to her feet, expecting him to help her out on to the jetty. But instead he stood silently regarding her.

Behind her, the sun had almost dropped into the Pacific, and the glorious streaks of colour were turning his face into molten gold, so that even his eyes were like those of a strange, glittering supernatural creature and each long black lash was tipped with a speck of gold dust.

Wordlessly, Sherry stared at him, feeling her insides

contract and tighten as though a giant hand had closed over them. If only she'd given in to him, everything would have been so different—she'd have stood beside him, laughing up at him, enclosed in his embrace while he dropped tender kisses on her head. And then they would have spent all night clasped in each other's arms. . .

But no—the fierce anger stirred in her again—she'd been right to resist him, and he, especially after what she'd told him, completely in the wrong. Oh, why couldn't he just have accepted that? Through his arrogance, his ruthless determination to take what he wanted, he'd ruined everything.

Angry, miserable tears burned her eyes. Of course, she'd have to give up her job. She couldn't possibly stay on with him for two whole years, with this tension smouldering between them like a barely-banked-down fire. Or maybe he'd already decided to dismiss her— make her join that no doubt long, ignominious list of women who'd failed to come up to Tyler Brennan's demanding expectations. In which case, for her pride's sake, she must get in first.

She took a couple of steps towards him. 'Tyler, I——'

But then her voice quavered into silence as he lifted a strand of silky hair which the evening breeze had blown across her face, tucked it behind her ear, then stood looking down at her, an expression on his face that she had never seen there before.

'Sherry.' His voice was not quite steady. 'There's only one way out of this.'

Alarm flared in her. 'W-what do you mean?'

'You must marry me.'

CHAPTER SEVEN

'What?'

Sherry's eyes were almost swallowing her face. She hadn't heard him correctly—she couldn't have.

'I said you must marry me,' Tyler repeated impatiently.

She gaped at him across the faintly rocking deck. 'You're crazy. Absolutely crazy.'

'Why am I so crazy? Back there on the island, you——'

'No,' she broke in. She didn't want to be reminded of anything she'd said—or so nearly done—back there. 'I suppose I should be flattered.'

'Flattered? Why, for heaven's sake?'

'For you to be prepared to go to these lengths, just to have me.'

'Oh, no, Sherry.' His voice dropped. 'We both know, don't we? We've known since the very first night we met. Married or not, it's only a matter of time—and not very much time—before we make love. We——'

'*No*,' she repeated loudly. 'That's not true.'

But he only smiled at her, and, lifting one hand, gently brushed his thumb across her lips, then brought it very slowly down her throat until it rested on the pulse at the base. And Sherry, desperately willing herself to stand unmoved under his insidious assault, felt the shudder of desire which ran through her, and knew that Tyler felt it too.

112

'Only a matter of time, Sherry,' he repeated, in a velvety purr.

Her will to resist him was being sapped, her body growing heavy with the longing to be in his arms again. In a final effort to break free, she jerked her head back violently.

'You realise that this is the third rule you've broken today?' she demanded.

He looked at her quizzically. 'The third?'

'Yes.' She ticked them off on her fingers. 'No pleasure with business. No Brennan relationships. And now this—I thought you were supposed to be permanently off marriage?'

'So did I.' He shook his head in apparent bewilderment, then ran his fingers through his hair. 'Tell me, are we Geminis affected by the full moon, by any chance?'

The daylight had faded with tropical suddenness, and he gestured towards the horizon from where a full silver moon had just slid upwards through the violet dusk, sending a shimmering trail across the sea to touch both their faces.

'Everybody's affected by it.' Sherry, still struggling to regain her composure, gave an all but inaudible reply.

'You mean I'm merely suffering from moon madness.' She heard the wry self-mockery in his voice.

'Yes. Very probably,' she replied in an expressionless tone. 'Tomorrow morning you'll regret ever having asked me.'

'Well, in that case, I don't intend chancing it. I want your answer now.'

Under his inexorable pressure, panic began to flood through her. 'But I don't——'

She'd been going to say 'love you' but bit back the words, terrified that she would unleash another deeply cynical response from him. Love, Sherry? And since when did love have anything to do with marriage? No, she couldn't bear to hear him say that.

And besides, if she refused him, they would never see each other again. And how could she bear that— the rest of her life without Tyler? An existence which would be a bleak, arid desert for her to drag herself painfully through. And that could mean only one thing—the dreadful realisation hit her like a blast of icy wind from the north. She loved him.

But could she—*dared* she give her heart to him?

'Don't what, Sherry?'

He was watching her intently. What had her face revealed? Hastily, she smoothed it into a blank mask.

'Don't—don't trust you,' she improvised. 'You must understand, Tyler. I-I just can't let myself trust any man, ever again.

'Oh, Sherry.' He reached for her, and she allowed herself to be drawn unresisting into his arms. His face against her hair, he said softly, 'I know you've had a hard time, but I promise that I'll make it up to you. And, whatever those other two Geminis were like, this one's different, I swear it.'

'Is he?' Pillowed against Tyler's chest, Sherry gave a small, sad smile. 'All this,' she whispered, 'just to sleep with me.'

'No, it isn't *just* to sleep with you.' He held her away from him, his fingers digging painfully into her shoulders. 'I've told you—a day, a week, and I'd achieve that.' And this time she did not even try to argue, for she knew it was the truth. 'But that's not enough, I want far, far more from you, Sherry, than that beautiful body. I want *you*.'

The look in his eyes was turning her insides to water. Unable to meet the fierce, overpowering blaze in them, she bent her head.

'But you don't know me, Tyler.' She paused, bewildered. Could it really only be a week since this man had swept into her life? 'We only met——'

He silenced her with a soft, throaty laugh. 'My sweet girl, I've known you all my life. It's just that I didn't happen to meet you until eight days ago. But that's irrelevant. If I know you for ten years, I'll still want to marry you, and as I'm not prepared to wait ten years, well, then——'

Very gently, he tilted her face up to his. In the pale moonlight she saw only tenderness; even those sardonic grey eyes were warm and silvery soft.

Oh, her mind wanted to battle on. Even now that she knew she loved him, she still shrank from entrusting herself to any man. No surrender, her mind screamed in her ear. If you don't fight him, Sherry, you'll live to regret this night's work.

But her body yearned to give in, and here—in the magic of a tropical night, with Tyler taking her in his arms, as he was doing now, running his lips softly down her cheek, then coming to rest over her ear, his tongue softly probing it with little darting thrusts so that she was closing her eyes and melting into his embrace— here, her body was winning the life and death battle.

'Do you really mean it?' she whispered.

He held her away from him again. 'Yes, I do,' he

replied sombrely. 'More than anything I've ever wanted in this world, I want to marry you.'

'Well, then——'

She gave him a tremulous smile, and saw the exultant gleam in his eyes as he gathered her into his arms. His mouth came down on hers and with a new, delicious thrill of freedom she opened hers to receive his tongue, moaning softly in her throat and sliding her arms round his back to press him to her, her soft pliant body yielding to his strong one.

This time, it was Tyler who broke the kiss. 'No.' Pushing her from him, he gave a shaken laugh. 'Oh, Sherry, what you do to me. But no more until we're married.'

She gave him a provocative little pout. 'And when will that be?'

'Tomorrow.'

'Tomorrow?' she squeaked. 'B-but that's impossible.'

'Why is it?' Tyler obviously saw no problem.

'But where?'

'Right here. The hotel can lay on everything, from your bouquet to the best man—although I aim to get Ed to fill that roll.'

So his quicksilver Gemini mind had already leapt on far ahead of hers.

'No, no, we can't,' she protested, but with a feeling of utter helplessness. She was being swept away down a flooded river, and desperately tried to cling to a branch of cold reality to save herself. 'We can't possibly arrange everything so quickly.'

'Of course we can. Have you got your birth certificate with you?'

'Well, yes. It's with my passport, along with my vaccination certificates.'

'That's it, then—no problem. Unless——' He stopped suddenly. 'Would you prefer to be married in England, if you've got family there?'

'There's only an elderly aunt and uncle, and I haven't seen them for ages,' Sherry admitted reluctantly, but still she tried to temporise. 'What about you? Wouldn't you rather get married in Los Angeles?'

He laughed wryly. 'Oh, yes, and have my brothers and a whole clutch of male cousins ogling my beautiful bride? No,' he said firmly. 'It's a wedding in paradise for us—tomorrow.'

CHAPTER EIGHT

BUT they were not married next day. Even Tyler was not able to manipulate the laws of Tahiti to suit himself to that extent. The marriage regulations had obstinately refused to bend, even in the face of his determined onslaught, and finally he'd had to accept that— though with a very ill grace.

And Sherry, remembering his scowl and the shocking temper he'd been in for the rest of that day, suppressed a little smile but then all at once the smile faded. She'd managed, at last, to smooth his angry plumage, but would she always be able to calm that Gemini temperament? Or would they spend the rest of their lives being whirled dizzily around by his mercurial nature, which changed from light to dark and back again to light almost before she could draw a steadying breath?

She stared at the reflection in her bathroom mirror, then, seeing that little vertical line of worry which had appeared between her arched brows, shook herself mentally. A fit of the glooms on her wedding-day?

She whispered softly to herself, 'Hello, Mrs Tyler Brennan,' felt her heart skip a beat, blushed, laughed, and was instantly transformed into a radiant bride.

'Sherry—are you awake?' The knock at the bungalow door and the soft voice roused her.

'Yes. Come in, Riva,' she called, and went through to the bedroom, just as the young woman entered, a large straw bag draped over her arm.

She gave Sherry a conspiratorial wink. 'I've banished Tyler. Ed's keeping a close eye on him—he's persuaded him that it's bad luck to see his bride on the wedding morning.'

'Yes, well, that's true,' Sherry replied solemnly.

In actual fact, she hadn't seen *that* much of Tyler over the last few days. That night, after his proposal, he'd burst into her bedroom, dressed for dinner, with the most perfunctory knocks, just as she emerged from the bathroom wrapped only in a towel. He'd backed out rapidly, been thoroughly irritable over dinner, then announced that he was moving out of the bungalow until the wedding. He couldn't, he'd said with a wry grimace, be answerable for his actions otherwise.

Riva rolled her eyes. 'I hope you're not as nervous as he is, Sherry. He's as twitchy as a kitten.'

Tyler, a kitten—and nervous? Sherry smiled at the thought, at the same time blessing the good fortune which had brought Ed, his oldest college friend, down to Tahiti for six weeks to research a book on ancient Polynesian settlements, then slyly introduced him to this sweet, gentle dark-eyed beauty, so that instantly he'd lost all interest in the vexed question of eastward or westward migration flows, married and settled down here for good.

Riva frowned as she eyed the breakfast tray which the maid had left almost an hour before. 'You haven't eaten a thing.'

Sherry pulled a face. 'Ugh. I couldn't manage a mouthful—I'm just not hungry.'

'Yes, you are.' The younger girl wagged a stern finger, then went over to the tray and poured a cup of coffee. 'As your bridesmaid, I will not have you fainting halfway through the ceremony. Whatever would Tyler say?'

'Oh, no—really,' Sherry wailed, but it was a half-hearted protest, and she allowed herself to be sat down in a chair while a little coffee, some orange juice and a few mouthfuls of croissant were forced down her throat.

Finally, she was released to go and bathe, and shampoo her hair. Then Riva, who before her own marriage had been a hairdresser in a hotel on Tahiti, settled her at the dressing-table, dried her hair and arranged it into a loose, shining knot at her nape, with just a few tendrils left to twine round the tiny circlet of white stephanotis which she carefully pinned to the top of her head.

'You know, Sherry, you are very lucky.' She spoke through a mouthful of hair-pins. 'I first met Tyler last year—he stayed with us for a few days. Oh, he can be—temperamental,' momentarily, their eyes met in shared acknowledgement, 'but he is a good man. I thought then, a difficult man to please, but the woman who captures his heart will be blessed indeed.'

But have I? All at once, a little cold finger of panic touched Sherry's spine. Have I really captured Tyler's heart, or is he, with this all but instant wedding, only acting out his role as Gemini man—impulsive, impetuous, but as changeable as the tides. . .?

Riva tilted Sherry's face and looked down at her critically. 'You're very pale.'

'Oh, just pre-wedding jitters,' Sherry muttered, through lips gone suddenly stiff with terror.

'Well, I'll give you a little blusher, and a touch of

this eye-shadow and mascara——' Riva was working deftly '—then just a coat of pink lip gloss.'

Was it too late? Could she send Riva out to tell Tyler that she'd changed her mind? He'd understand—— Oh, who are you kidding? You'd never get off the island with a whole skin. Of course it's too late—and anyway, you love him, don't you?

Yes, I do, she silently told her anxious reflection. And suddenly she knew. It was as if, for the first time, she saw into the very depths of her heart and knew that for the rest of her life, whatever else might happen, she would love Tyler, deeply and passionately.

'All right now, Sherry?'

Behind her, Riva too was watching her reflection and she gave her a dazzling smile. 'All right—and thank you.'

There was a discreet cough from the veranda. Riva went out and came back with two bouquets—her own, of pink orchid buds and hibiscus, and Sherry's sweetly perfumed posy of white stephanotis and gardenia blossoms, enclosed in a circle of glossy green leaves.

'Time to get dressed,' she warned, and turned to the wardrobe.

Sherry had tried to insist that a pretty, calf-length dress of white Indian cotton in the hotel boutique would be perfect for a tropical wedding, but Tyler had had other ideas. She'd finally given in—of course— only remarking caustically that she thought it was supposed to be her wedding as well as his, but he had simply given her that maddening smile and kissed the tip of her nose, before whisking her off to Tahiti.

Having peremptorily dismissed every ready-made wedding-dress on the entire island, he'd bought a bolt

of heavy pearl-white silk then tracked down the island's
top dressmaker.

When Sherry, terrified that she'd end up with
nothing to wear, had protested mutinously that she'd
far rather choose her own wedding-dress, and anyway
she'd very much liked that one in the last shop they'd
been in, Tyler had scowled—not for the first time that
day—and silenced her with the information that in
Tahiti the bridegroom always bought his bride's dress.

It had arrived on the last flight the evening before
and Sherry, with a superstitious certainty that it would
have to be the white Indian cotton after all, had just
slipped it on to check that it fitted, deliberately not
allowing herself to look in the mirror, then put it
quickly away.

Now she watched as Riva got it off its hanger then
she stepped into it, standing motionless as the girl drew
it up around her and fastened all the tiny pearl buttons.
Finally, she took a long look at herself in the full-
length mirror, then they both gazed at each other,
round-eyed.

The dressmaker must be a sorceress. Only someone
with supernatural powers could, on the strength of one
swift and seemingly casual measurement of Sherry's
height, bust and hips, have produced such a miracle of
a dress from a few metres of inanimate fabric.

Slightly waisted, long-sleeved, the tight bodice set
off her high breasts and slender waist before falling to
a slim, full-length skirt which subtly emphasised the
curve of her hips and the long line of her thighs and
legs. She moved a fraction, and the dress came alive,
shimmering and rustling slightly.

Riva gave it a final twitch, then exclaimed, 'Oh, honey, you look wonderful.'

And Sherry, her eyes like stars, biting her lip, could only give her a rather tremulous smile.

Perching herself on the bed, she watched while Riva peeled off her sundress and fetched out from the straw bag her pink silk blouse and matching flowered *pareu*— both bought by Tyler, of course—and put them on.

Riva was pulling a comb through her black, gleaming hair when there was another knock, and she peeped out through the shutters.

'Oh, it's Uncle James.' Whirling across to the door, she flung it open. 'Come on in—we're ready.'

James Sylvester, Ed's grey-haired bachelor uncle, came in, rather shyly. 'Morning, Riva; morning, Sherry.'

Soon after Ed and Riva married, he had visited them and impulsively—the first thing in his life he'd ever done on impulse, Ed had assured Sherry—thrown up a thriving law practice in San Francisco and settled down here. Now, stiff and uncomfortable-looking in a cream suit, he had been hijacked by Tyler and his nephew into giving her away.

'Ready, ladies? Well. . .' he cleared his throat, '. . . let's go.'

And, dream-like, Sherry took the posy which Riva held out to her, its sensuous perfume in her nostrils almost her last grip on reality, and followed them out into the shady gardens. . .

Ever after, for Sherry, her wedding-day would be like a film, very slightly blurred at the edges and out of focus. . . Smiling faces, other hotel guests and staff watching her progress. . . Someone lifting her skirt slightly for her to climb the steps which led into the main complex. . .

The room where the ceremony was to take place, which had been a perfectly ordinary room when she'd peeped in the day before, was now transformed into a scented bower, flowers in every corner, on every surface: tall jars of white lilies, arching wreaths of pink bougainvillaea, and bowls of white stephanotis which echoed her posy, set among the candles on the table where the priest was waiting.

And Tyler. He was waiting too, watching her as she came towards him down the red carpet, which had surely also appeared since yesterday. His eyes were shuttered of expression but there was a tightness around his lips and a tension in his whole body which somehow belied the cool assurance of his pale grey suit and immaculate white shirt.

As she came up to him, he stared down at her then gave her a funny little smile which made her lungs contract. The priest cleared his throat and they both turned to him. . .

Afterwards, out on the lawn, the solemnity of the ceremony relaxed, there was—not confetti but real flowers heads, handfuls of them, so that they both seemed to be standing in a sea of crushed petals. . .

And the photographs. . . '*Please* turn this way, Mrs Brennan.'

Sherry, lost in a pink haze, vaguely heard the photographer's agitated request, then gave a quick, startled blush as she realised whom he meant. Tyler came up to her, slid one arm round her waist to rest possessively over her hip.

'Hi, there, Mrs Brennan. Having problems with your new name?'

He smiled into her eyes, and she realised that for the first time in days that tautness had gone. His mouth was relaxed, all the old indolence back. Had he perhaps been afraid that she wouldn't go through with it? Of course not—why should he? Surely, everything always went Tyler's way. All the same, she slid her hand into his.

'You know something, Mrs Brennan?' he murmured. 'You are quite the most beautiful woman I've ever met.'

'Kiss your bride, please, Mr Brennan,' chirruped the photographer's assistant and he obliged, with a long, lingering kiss which brought ribald comments from some of the male guests.

He drew back his head at last and gazed down at her, the expression in his eyes so intent that it set Sherry's pulse flickering with suppressed excitement.

'Definitely the most beautiful—and the most desirable,' he added huskily.

Somehow, she managed a teasing smile. 'Oh? But what about that Sherry Southwell I've seen you with?'

'Ah—Ms Southwell.' Tyler shook his head. 'A sad disappointment. She started out so well, but turned into such a scratchy, *difficult* young woman that in the end she just had to go.'

'Why, you——!' Laughing with outrage, she brought up her posy and thumped him in the solar-plexus with it, just as the camera clicked again.

'That's a prime one for the family album, Ty,' Ed, if anything even more laconic than Tyler, called across. 'Something to show all your kids.'

Sherry, absurdly blushing again, gratefully allowed the assistant to draw her away to be posed against a bank of pink and mauve bougainvillaea.

'Turn your head a little, Mrs Brennan. . . Bouquet up a fraction, Mrs Brennan. . . Look down, Mrs Brennan.'

A purple floweret drifted to the ground. She stared at it, seeing instead another one fall on to her naked stomach and Tyler's hand capturing it, circling her bare midriff with it. . . And then she saw once more that cascading screen of flowers, which she'd parted with her fingers and glimpsed the waterfall—and Tyler, standing beside it——

Abruptly, she jerked out of her daydream, looked up and across the lawn, over the heads of the guests, to see his eyes fixed on hers, a message in them for her alone—a message which made her pulses flicker again, her blood first slow then gallop uncontrollably.

And then he was leading her into the shady, flower-filled restaurant, for the sumptuous wedding lunch. More photographs. . .half-heard snatches of conversation. . .happy laugher. . . But all that was on the very periphery of her being; all her consciousness was fused into the man sitting beside her, his leg brushing casually against hers, his sleeve touching her hand as he leaned forward to speak to someone across the table.

Champagne. . . toasts. . . the cake—Tyler standing just behind her, his hand closing over hers as she gripped the knife. . . the band arriving, so that the dancing could begin.

Then Tyler, after only the second dance, edged them away into the garden again and, putting up his finger to silence her, led her out of sight behind the flowering shrubs.

'But we can't leave yet,' she protested.

'Sure we can. They're all having a great time—they won't miss us.'

'Oh.' She returned his smile rather hesitantly, then ran her tongue around her lips. They'd hardly been on their own together for days, and here she was, quite alone with this man who was now her husband, his hand firmly clasped over hers, drawing her away from her old existence into a new, uncertain life with him.

As though sensing her inner turbulence, he was walking faster and faster so that, clutching up her silk skirt with her free hand, she had to run to keep up with him.

Not speaking, he led her through the grounds, past the turning for their bungalow and down towards the sea. When they reached the jetty, Sherry gasped as she saw, resting at anchor, the most beautiful sailing ship she had ever seen. The sleek white hull glistened in the late afternoon sun and smartly uniformed sailors were busy unfurling the huge sails.

But were they——? Sherry turned questioning eyes to Tyler and he said, with the glimmer of a smile, 'That's right—a honeymoon at sea. Ideal for a Piscean, don't you agree?'

A crew member helped her down on to the deck, then they alone stood together at the prow, the white sails flapping softly overhead, the warm breeze on their faces and whipping at her dress, as a dozen tiny offshore islands slipped past. Gradually, the light faded and the sun slid down behind a bank of cloud; the sky turned to scarlet, then crimson, then exquisite peach, and finally, as the tropical night closed in, to palest moon-drenched gold.

'Mmmm.' Sherry, nestled contentedly against Tyler, broke a silence which had lasted at least an hour. 'There can't ever have been a sunset quite so wonderful. It was—oh, it was like something out of *South Pacific*.'

She sighed again and behind her Tyler laughed softly. 'Well, I'm afraid I can't conjure up Rossano Brazzi for you, but will I do instead?'

Clasping her wrists, he turned her slowly round to him until they stood, just inches apart. His face was all but invisible, but she sensed the desire uncoiling itself in him.

'Hungry?' he asked softly.

'N-no.'

'Well, I am,' he said throatily, and she knew that he did not mean for food.

Putting his arm round her, he drew her down the private staircase and into a large cabin, almost submerged in flowers, and luxuriously furnished with dressing-table, armchairs, and a wide double bed—Sherry's eyes rested on it for a moment, then skittered away.

Beyond, she glimpsed a bathroom, all cream and gold fittings, while, by the soft light of the pink-shaded wall lamps, she could see her clothes hanging in the half-open wardrobe—and on the bed lay one of her still unworn nightdresses and its matching négligé.

'A bit of fancy footwork by Riva and one of the maids during that endless photo session,' Tyler remarked.

'Oh.' Sherry found that she could not quite meet his

eye. 'What a beautiful cabin this is—you'd hardly believe you were on a boat. And what lovely flowers——'

'Stop babbling.'

'Sorry.'

It was all she could trust herself to say. Shyness with this man, who was still almost a stranger, was gripping her so that she could barely move. Hesitantly, she put her hand to the pearl buttons on her nape, but he pushed it aside.

'I'll do it.'

She felt his fingers, warm against her skin, then very slowly he unhooked the buttons. His hands were very, very slightly unsteady, and Sherry realised suddenly that he was holding himself in check, taut as a drawn bowstring.

And all at once her own shyness melted away. She turned round and lifted her arms from her sides.

'You take it off for me.'

Their eyes met, then Tyler, his fingers brushing softly against the fine hairs on her arms so that the skin tingled under his touch, very slowly eased the tight sleeves and drew the dress down past her waist, going on to his haunches to pull it over her hips, her knees, until it lay like sea foam at her feet.

She stepped out of it and he took it, tossing it over a chair back. As he straightened up, his gaze took in the creamy silk bra and pants, and his eyes, suddenly very dark, lingered over the high swell of her breasts and the long tender line of her hips and legs.

'I was beginning to think you'd made a vow never to wear them.' Behind his casual words there was a husky throb which set her blood racing ever more erratically.

'What better occasion than my wedding-day?' she murmured demurely.

'But even so, too many clothes for such a hot night.'

She stood motionless, one hand to her throat, as he unclipped her bra and pulled it away from her, so that her freed breasts fell into his cupped hands. Then, stooping again, he slid the silk panties down past her thighs until she could step out of them.

He remained where he was, on his haunches, looking up at her, an expression on his face which set up, very deep inside her, a soft trembling like a harp string vibrating in the wind.

'Kneeling at my feet, Tyler?' She tried to keep her voice light, but a betraying tremor came through in it.

He gave her that soft, panther's smile which she knew so well. 'At you feet, Sherry—paying homage to your beauty. Has anyone ever told you how very beautiful you are—and how desirable?'

'Only one,' she murmured dreamily. 'Just a few hours ago——'

'Sssh.'

Very slowly, he slid possessive hands up her long legs until he held her by her hips, his fingers splayed in the soft flesh. His tongue circled the hollow of her navel, slowly, erotically, until with a gasp she clutched wildly at his thick thatch of black hair, twining and retwining, while, as his mouth went lower across her abdomen, the sensations ripped through her.

Now, at last, she was free to surrender to her longing for him. He was right. Since the moment of their first meeing it had been between them, a promise, and now, as the aching need to have that promise fulfilled welled up in her, she slid to her knees, her face in his hair.

'Please, Tyler.'

It was no more than the faintest sigh, but he heard it and raised his head, his eyes black in the half-light. He stared at her for a moment, as though he could not quite focus on her, then, with a low growl deep in his throat, dragged her into his arms, bearing her down beneath him on to the soft, springy carpet, crushing her body as he moved across her.

Next instant, as if possessed by some demon, he had thrust her thighs apart and was driving into her yielding body with a savage, raw urgency which made her gasp aloud with shock, her dilated eyes staring blindly at the cabin ceiling.

As he began to move in her, exquisite pleasure, a hair's breadth away from pain, made her cry out again and dimly she heard Tyler's muttered response. But the pleasure was unbearable; it was so intense that she must die. The fire of his passion was flaring inside her, the answering flames burning with an incandescent white heat. Surely she would be seared to the bone, her flesh consumed until there was nothing left but dead ashes.

And then, just as she hovered on the very brink of extinction for ever, the flames fused into a fireball, exploded and sent her tumbling back to earth, scorched, changed irrevocably from the old Sherry, but still—miraculously—alive.

At long last, Tyler raised his head from where it lay on her breast and they stared wordlessly into each other's eyes, both shaken to their roots by that firestorm of passion.

'Well, Mrs Brennan?' He tried to sound flippant, but then the half-smile faded and catching up her hand he gently brushed his lips across the palm. 'Oh, my sweet, I knew we'd be good together—but I never dreamed it could be like this.'

And Sherry, still too shattered to find words, softly caressed his cheek. 'I love you, Tyler.'

'And I love you,' he replied sombrely, but even as her heart leapt with joy he shook his head in disbelief. 'I've never said that to another woman—never thought I *could* love. But don't ever leave me, Sherry—I couldn't live without you.' He gave a rueful grimace which was only half joking. 'And I'm not at all sure that I like hearing myself say that.'

'In that case, don't say it.' She gave him a provocative look from under her lashes. 'If you really love me—well, show me.'

'With the greatest of pleasure.'

But even as he went to draw her to him again, she gasped, her eyes rounded with horror as she saw the ring of bluish bruises on his left shoulder and surely—yes, those were teeth marks, one little pinprick even oozing a drop of blood.

'I'm s-sorry,' she whispered shamedly.

But he said quickly, 'Don't look like that, my sweet—I loved you that way, my darling little she-cat.'

Putting his thumb under her chin, he tilted her face to his. 'Tell me, Sherry—has it ever been like that for you before?'

'No—never.' She hesitated, then went on slowly, 'Piers was my only lover, and he——' she frowned, trying to remember; it was all another lifetime ago '—he never seemed very bothered about how I felt.'

'Good.' He spoke with savage satisfaction. 'I'm glad

that swine didn't have the intelligence to discover what he had under his hand. I want to teach you myself— although,' he flashed her a teasing grin, 'you seemed to be doing very nicely without any instruction from me.'

She felt herself colouring again but he went on, his fingers tightening on her, 'Oh, my sweet, let's start from now—a voyage of discovery for us both. You know,' he gave her a slanting, sideways smile, 'ever since I laid eyes on you that first night, I've fantasised over where we'd first make love. Usually it was some marvellous tropical beach, but I must admit my fantasies never stretched quite as far as a cabin carpet.'

And, catching her up in his arms, he laid her down on the cool silk sheet, and came down beside her. . .

Hours later, after sensual, passionate lovemaking which left them both at the same time drowned yet avid for more, Sherry lay in a blissful stupor, the scent of him on her skin, the imprint of his flesh on and in her flesh.

Beside her, Tyler had finally fallen asleep, a lock of tousled black hair flopped over his forehead, the taut lines round his eyes and mouth relaxed into peace, his mouth curved into the smile of a sated panther.

As she smoothed away that lock of hair, she heard him murmur softly then fall into a deeper slumber. Then she too, lulled by the gentle motion of the boat, let herself drift into sleep, a sensuous little smile hovering round her lips. . .

When she roused, a pale shaft of light was filtering in through one of the portholes. Her eyes opened wide in puzzlement then, as she felt an arm lying possessively across her, memory flooded back. She yawned, stretched gingerly, and felt the delicious languor which permeated her entire body.

The arm was heavy and inert—Tyler must still be sound asleep. Very carefully—for he would sleep like a cat, she didn't doubt—she slid away then, slipping on the cream silk négligé which, like its matching nightdress, had remained unworn, slowly stood up.

The cabin was still filled with the fragrance of flowers. She bent to sniff at one of the bowls of white gardenia then, on impulse, took a flower head, brushed aside her tangled hair and tucked it behind her ear.

Very quietly, she let herself out into the corridor and went up their private steps to emerge on deck. All around her was silence, apart from the faint throb of the engine far below, the rustle of sails above and the cool morning breeze on her face.

Over in the east the sky was a water-colour palette of softest apricot and aquamarine. As she stood at the prow, gripping the rail, she saw the dawn light glinting palely on the wide gold band on her finger. She was—she really was—Tyler's wife.

'Good morning, Mrs Brennan.' Behind her, Tyler put his arms round her, drawing her back against his body. 'Sleep well?'

'Mmmm. Wonderfully, thank you.' She could scarcely keep the bubbling happiness out of her voice.

'Strange—so did I. It must have been the sea air,' he responded gravely.

He turned her round to face him, then when he saw the flower nestling behind her ear, gave her a mock-scowl. 'And what exactly do you think you're up to, Mrs Brennan?'

She gave him a provocative look. 'Behind the right ear—that means I've got a lover.'

'Wrong.' He removed the gardenia unceremoniously, 'Right ear—you *want* a lover; left—you've found one. So. . .' He tucked the offending flower in place. 'And I intend to make sure that you never, ever want a lover. Except one, that is.'

He gave her a look which made her insides tremble, but even so she could not stop herself blurting out uncertainly, 'Will you always be my lover, Tyler?'

'Will I go on breathing till I die?' he responded, all laughter gone. 'Oh, Sherry, I knew from the first I had to have you. Whatever the cost, you had to be mine.'

You had to be mine. The Gemini male—ruthless, utterly determined to get what he considered rightfully his. A little *frisson* of unease crinkled the skin on her spine, and Tyler drew her close.

'Not cold, are you?'

It would be all right, wouldn't it? Of course it would. What had he said? It was just an accident of birth that had made him a Gemini. Far, far more than that, he was himself, Tyler.

As though he had caught something of her thoughts, he murmured softly in her ear, 'I'll love you, my darling, for ever and ever, for all eternity. But just in case you still have any doubts. . .'

He loosed one of his hands and drew from the pocket of his canvas shorts a tiny box. Flicking it open, he took out a ring and taking hold of her left hand slid it down to rest against her wedding-ring.

'Oh, it's beautiful,' Sherry exclaimed, turning her hand this way and that so that the stone, a dull, tawny brown, veined with gold which echoed the heavy gold setting, could catch the light. 'What kind of stone is it?'

'Agate. It's only semi-precious, but as soon as I saw it I knew that was the one for you—it perfectly matches your eyes.'

'It's really lovely, thank you.' She smiled up at him, soft-eyed. 'But you didn't need to buy me a ring—not with such a short engagement.'

'I'll buy you just what I choose,' he replied brusquely. 'After all, what are wives for if not to be covered from head to foot in jewels by their adoring husbands? But if you'd rather, we'll call it an eternity ring.'

'But when did you buy it?'

'While you were being measured for your dress, I slipped back to the goldsmith where we got your wedding-ring. At the same time, I put in a rush order for them to make this.'

This time, from his pocket he produced a slightly larger box and when she stared down at it wonderingly, he said, with a hint of impatience, 'Well, open it.'

She obeyed, then gave a little gasp of astonishment. Nestling in a bed of white velvet was a gold bracelet and as, with slightly shaking fingers, she lifted it up, she saw the matching fish, with glistening diamond eyes, hanging from it.

'A wedding present for a Piscean.' He gave a slight grimace. 'I seem to remember you lost one rather like it not long ago.'

'Y-yes, I think I did. It's beautiful, Tyler. Thank you—but even so, you——'

'Sssh.' He took her wrist and clicked the bracelet

into place, then held up her arm so that the fish swung free, gleaming in the early morning light.

As she nestled into him again, she murmured, 'What are we doing today?'

'See that island ahead? That's what we're making for. We'll be rowed ashore, the boat will anchor a discreet distance away and we'll spend the day there—quite alone. A picnic on the beach, swimming in the lagoon——'

'Oh—did Riva remember to pack my swim-suit?'

'Now why,' he nibbled gently at her ear, 'should you think you'll need such a thing as a swim-suit?'

She hesitated, as a wisp or two of the old shyness drifted back, and he shook his head reprovingly. 'You know, I seem to remember that that Ms Southwell, in a previous existence, of course, had no such inhibitions.' And Sherry laughed and relaxed.

She looked up at him. The low sun was gilding his face, turning him into a god again. But a very earthly god, she thought, remembering the night they had shared, and a flicker of desire ran through her veins.

A flock of white birds wheeled overhead and she sighed with utter contentment.

'Oh, how marvellous it all is. I wish this could go on forever.'

'Well. . .' Tyler pulled a face. 'It can go on for the next five days, but then it's back to earth, I'm afraid. I've got a group of architects and landscape designers flying down from the States to begin work on the hotel.'

'So we'll be in Bora Bora for some time?' Sherry's heart, which had plummeted slightly, lilted again.

'Yes. Several weeks at least. And then I plan a little island-hopping.'

'Around Polynesia, you mean?'

'Not exactly, no. First stop Sri Lanka—our hotel there is badly in need of a shake-up—then Mauritius—I'm looking to expand our operations there—and then the Bahamas.'

'Oh.' Sherry felt giddy at the thought. While Tyler's eyes were gleaming at the prospect of so much high-speed, high-powered travel, she had the feeling that over the next few weeks and months she was going to feel like nothing so much as a pebble, sent skimming and bouncing across a pond.

Only the ponds were going to be oceans, and the landing points—dazedly, she ticked them off in her mind—Sri Lanka, Mauritius, the Bahamas. . .

CHAPTER NINE

AND LOS ANGELES, where the pebble had finally come
to rest. Sherry sat at her desk, supposedly checking
through the agenda for the next Brennan board meeting, but in reality staring out from the fifteenth-storey
picture window of her office across the smoggy
cityscape.

She sighed faintly. More and more lately, she was
finding herself wishing that that pebble could have
gone on bouncing forever. They'd only been back here
six weeks, but Tyler was day by day growing more
moody, more irritable with everyone around him,
including—no, she had to face it, especially with her.

Could it possibly be that he——? Sherry abruptly
closed her mind to what his frequent outbursts might
mean, and picked up a pen.

Along the plush-carpeted corridor a door—Tyler's
door, she thought, her automatic reflexes leaping into
action—opened.

'Sherry!' The pen slipped from her fingers and rolled
away off the desk. 'Sherry—where the hell are you?'

She scrambled to her feet, but before she could move
her office door burst open and Tyler, in his shirtsleeves,
sparks flying almost visibly in all directions, erupted
through it.

'So there you are.'

He crossed the carpet in three strides then stood,
just the other side of her desk, glowering at her.

Running the tip of her tongue round her ash-dry lips, she asked feebly, 'Did you want something, Tyler?'

'Do I want something?' he exclaimed. 'Well, right now I'd settle for your head on a platter.'

Sherry, feeling her legs giving way beneath her, slid hastily down into her chair. But that was a mistake—it only allowed Tyler to stand over her, browbeating her even more. He brought both his bunched fists down hard on the desk and leaned on them, breathing deeply.

'Correct me if I'm wrong,' his voice had undergone a swift change from red-hot fury to an ice-cold anger which made her stomach churn, 'but I was under the impression that you were my PA.'

'Y-yes, of course I am,' she replied, terrified of what was coming next.

'In that case perhaps—if it's not too much trouble, that is—you could explain—purely as my PA, of course—why I've just had a call from Sullivan Airlines enquiring why I hadn't arrived for a top-level meeting scheduled for,' he shot back his cuff and glanced cursorily at his gold wristwatch, 'ten, no, eleven minutes ago, with their joint managing director—a meeting which I knew nothing about but which was, I'm assured, fixed yesterday with my PA.'

Sherry gave a violent start and her eyes flew guiltily to the scribble in the memo pad beside her. But he was too quick for her and, even as she tried to slide her elbow across it, he snatched it up.

'Tuesday ten-thirty a.m. Meeting Sullivan Airlines,' he read out, then tossed it back down on to the desk.

'I'm sorry, Tyler,' she whispered miserably. 'I

couldn't get at your diary. You were in conference with the new finance director——'

'And that's supposed to be a valid reason?' He scowled down at her. 'I've spent a month trying to set up this link with them—an exclusive package for their aircraft to fly guests to our hotels worldwide—good for Sullivan, good for Brennan. And single-handed you've blown it for me. What kind of goddamn bunch of amateurs does this make us out to be?'

Sherry bit back a rising sob. 'I'm really sorry, Tyler.'

'And so am I.' He spoke, she registered with icy chill, as coolly, as impersonally as though she were a piece of the office furniture. 'You know, this just isn't good enough. It's not what I expect from a Brennan employee.'

Employee! Sherry opened her mouth but then closed it again. That was the way Tyler saw her—at least, from nine till five-thirty each day—and until now the way she'd insisted on being treated during office hours.

'And I still haven't forgotten that double-booking fiasco last week,' Sherry's hands clenched convulsively together under the desk, 'even if you have.'

'Actually, I haven't,' she muttered.

The memory of Tyler's face when the two rival corporate designers arrived simultaneously at his office door with their portfolios of sketches for the new Brennan house uniforms which he was commissioning was still seared on her memory. He'd smoothed things over in his usual suave, ultra-charming manner but then, as soon as they'd gone, had come storming down the corridor yelling, 'Sherry—I want a word with you.' And in fact he'd had quite a few words with her.

Then, a couple of days before that, there'd

been——Terrified that he was going to trawl through all her misdeeds, she blurted out again, 'All I can say is, I'm sorry.'

He stared down at her, then ran his fingers through his rumpled black hair. 'Look, what the hell's getting into you, Sherry?'

'I don't know,' she whispered, her head lowered. 'Perhaps Los Angeles doesn't suit me.'

He gave a brief, mirthless laugh. 'Or maybe you don't suit LA. You know what they say—if you can't stand the heat get out of the kitchen. Only in your case maybe you'd better get into the kitchen.'

Her head jerked up and she saw him still gazing down at her, his eyes narrowed.

'That night in Bristol, you seemed such an efficient, unflappable young woman, but I'm beginning to wonder if it was such a great idea to employ someone on the strength of two hours' acquaintance.'

Tears stung her eyes as the pain went through her like a knife wound to the heart—but she wouldn't let him see how much his words had hurt her. She met his gaze head-on, tossing back her silky hair proudly.

'Well, perhaps you should have left me in Bristol, then. At least I was happy there.'

'Maybe I should have done just that.'

He swung on his heel, but she couldn't let him leave like this, the anger still flaring between them.

'Wait a minute, Tyler. *Please*,' as he halted reluctantly. 'Would you like me to ring Sullivan? Explain that it was my fault, and try to——'

'No, thanks. I'll do it myself. That way I'll know it's done properly.'

When he had gone, Sherry sat for a long time,

staring at a corner of her green leather blotter. She couldn't blind herself any longer. As Tyler had just reminded her so brutally, he'd taken her on as his PA on two hours' acquaintance—but he'd married her on not much more. And now he was regretting it.

His growing moodiness and irritability, his savage outbursts of temper. Oh, he might cover them up as being caused by her mistakes at work—and goodness knew there'd been enough of them lately. Just what was wrong with her? She'd always been so capable, super-efficient, until now. Maybe it was true what she'd said about Los Angeles—she really had been feeling increasingly unwell these last few weeks.

I'll love you, my darling, for ever and ever, for all eternity. She looked down at her hands and realised that she was twisting the agate ring spasmodically. He'd meant it, she was quite sure he had, but eternity for him had lasted—what? All of five months. Regretting. . . regretting. The word went round and round in her head like a stuck needle on a record. A tropical moon—his driving sexual desire for her—the Gemini impulsiveness. All three ingredients had fizzed together into a lethal cocktail that night and now, quite simply, he was regretting their marriage.

'Are you all right, Mrs Brennan?' She roused herself to see one of the secretaries looking down at her in concern. 'You're very pale.'

'Oh.' Sherry struggled to put her face together into the semblance of a smile. 'I'm fine, Margie.'

The big, open-plan secretarial area was right next door to her office—and Tyler hadn't exactly kept his voice down. No doubt the entire Brennan building would know about their row—or rather, their latest row—inside an hour, and probably the entire Brennan empire by five-thirty this evening.

'I'm all right—really,' she said firmly, as the girl continued to stare at her.

'Good. Well—er—Mr Brennan asked me to let you know,' Margie's eyes did not quite meet hers, 'that he's gone out—he won't be back for lunch.'

'Thank you, Margie. Oh, and would you file these papers for me? They're to go under Finance.'

Fleetingly, Sherry became her old, efficient self but as soon as the door closed—very softly, as though she were an invalid—she gave up all pretence and, leaping up from her chair, went over to the window to stand gazing out, letting her eyes drift listlessly from one building to another, then back again. Regretting. . . regretting. The word filled her mind, was written on her brain in letters of fire.

Finally, after a long time, she picked up her bag and went into the washroom. Margie was right—she *was* very pale, all her suntan gone. Now, her skin was almost transparent, her brown eyes huge above those black coal-dust smudges.

Automatically, she combed her hair, reapplied pink lipstick and then blusher. But those two intense rosy spots on her cheeks made her look like a clown, so she scrubbed them off again, then went through to the secretarial area.

'Margie, I——' she was horribly aware of a dozen pairs of interested eyes and ears '—I think I'll go home. I've got a bit of a headache.'

And, before the girl could offer the warm sympathy which would have made the hard icy knot in her chest thaw into a flood of tears, she turned hastily away. . .

'Let me call you a cab, Mrs Brennan.'

So it had already reached as far as the ground floor, Sherry thought ironically, as the burly doorman tenderly shepherded her across the marble-floored entrance hall.

'No, thank you, Frank.' This time she managed quite an effective smile. 'I want to walk down to the Plaza, so I'll get a cab from there.'

She stood in the swing doors, gazing unseeingly at the back-to-front gilt lettering of 'Brennan International Group' on the glass in front of her, then stepped out just as the panel behind her clipped her heels. . .

She let herself into Tyler's—for that was how she always thought of it—luxury apartment, dumped her purchases on the kitchen table and opened the fridge door, meaning to get herself a late lunch. But somehow, in spite of that dreadful hollow feeling inside her, the thought of food, even just an omelette and green salad, set her stomach heaving.

Finally, she made a cup of coffee and, kicking off her high-heeled shoes, sat at the breakfast bar nibbling a dry cracker. Listlessly, she allowed her eyes to roam around the room. Luxury everywhere: gleaming, high-tech stainless steel fittings and units, immaculate slatted blinds. When he'd first brought her back here, Tyler had told her casually to change anything she didn't like, anything at all. Then he'd snatched her up in his arms—she'd been standing right there by the table—and carried her through to the bedroom. . .

Sherry closed her eyes against the images and then, quite out of the blue, a pang of yearning so intense

that it made her physically tremble went through her—
a yearning to be back in her pine kitchen in Bristol,
with the second-hand fridge-freezer with its rusting
hinges, the cutlery drawer that always jammed.

As ridiculous tears brimmed in her eyes, she thought
angrily, You fool, pining for a pine kitchen? Giggling
hysterically at the pun, she pushed away her lukewarm
coffee, carried her bag of purchases into the sitting-
room and huddled on one corner of the long cream
velvet-covered sofa.

Scrabbling in the carrier-bag, she fetched out the box
of chocolates she'd bought—English chocolates, as a
little treat—and tore off the wrapper. She ate a hazel-
nut cluster, followed by a vanilla fudge, but then, as
the queasiness in her stomach turned to very definite
nausea, closed the box and pushed it away.

She reached into the bag again and took out the fat
paperback book she'd bought in the pharmacy: *Your
Stars—Your Personality*. She'd stared at it guiltily for
several minutes, read the blub, then hastily paid for it
and crammed it into her bag.

Now, she opened it and began flicking idly through
the pages. 'Astrology, science of the ancients. . . The
major sun signs. . . Calculate your birth chart.' Sherry
paused, then read on. 'Your birth sign—Aries, Taurus
and so on—can only give you a simplified picture of
the typical personality traits of your group. Far more
important is the 'rising sign' constellation which was
ascendant at the precise time of your birth, for this can
strengthen, weaken or completely overshadow the
effect of your birth sign. To calculate any individual's
birth chart, all you need are——'

The sound of the apartment door opening made her

jump. She heard Tyler's purposeful stride in the hall and, just in time before he reached the open sitting-room doorway, she jammed the book under the nearest cushion.

He stood looking across at her, his lips tight, then advanced into the room, hurling his executive case down into a chair. So he was still in a foul mood. Sherry unwound her legs from under her and went to scramble to her feet.

'There's no need to move on my account.'

'But I'll get dinner started. I-I'm sorry—you're earlier than I expected, or I——'

'I don't want a meal,' he said brusquely. 'I'm going out training.'

'Oh?' She sank back on to the sofa, looking up at him questioningly.

'For next month's charity marathon, of course.' His voice crackled with irritation. 'Or is that something else you've forgotten?'

Sherry winced, but the biting sarcasm at least lashed her into some sort of response.

'No, of course I haven't. Although, if I had, it's only what you'd expect of me, isn't it?' The defiant words trembled though, and when she looked up at him it was through a sheen of tears.

Tyler muttered something under his breath, then, 'Oh, Sherry.'

He crossed the room and pulled her up into his arms, cradling her to him, stroking her hair as though she were a hurt child. At last he held her away from him, looking down into her eyes, his own face sombre.

'Sherry——' He broke off abruptly then gave her a rueful smile. 'We're just not making out, are we?'

'W-what do you mean?' Terror had her by the throat, draining the blood from her face.

'Working together—being together all the time.'

'Oh.'

A little sound, half-relief, half-sob, escaped from her and he drew her against him once more before going on rapidly, almost as though he had already planned what he was going to say, 'Living in each other's pockets all the time, day and night—well, it's creating problems for both of us, isn't it?'

'I suppose so.' Her voice was muffled against his jacket. 'And yet on our honeymoon you said——'

'Ah, yes. On our honeymoon.' She heard the wry smile in his voice. 'But that was before I tried it. You must understand, Sherry, all my life—my adult life— I've been a free agent, and now——'

And now he had a wife. Oh, he didn't say it, he didn't have to. But surely that was what he meant?

She freed herself from his embrace and looked directly at him. 'Just what are you trying to tell me, Tyler?'

He drew one deep breath. 'What I'm trying to tell you is that it will be better all round if I find myself a new PA.'

'*What*?'

Sherry stared up at him, stunned into silence beyond that one strangled word, and he seized on her silence.

'It really will be much better this way, darling. You'll see.'

'Oh, who for? You or me?' She had found a voice— a voice with a new razor edge. 'Well?' As he looked down at her silently, 'Answer me.'

He shook his head, half angry, half exasperated.

'For both of us, of course. Look, sweetie. . .' He lifted a finger to gently stroke her cheek but she jerked her head back. He frowned slightly but then went on evenly, 'You're my wife, and a Brennan wife simply does not have to work. They just have to be decorative—or, in your case, very decorative.'

He gave her a teasing smile, which made her ache to respond, but she would not. 'So that's all I am, is it? A decoration—an empty-headed bauble like—like a fairy on a Christmas tree—but not safe to be let loose anywhere near your office.'

'Oh, for——'

'And what do you think the rest of the Brennan staff will think?'

'Why should they think anything?'

His careless tone outraged her even more, 'Why should——? Oh, come on, Tyler. I know I've done some stupid things lately, but I'm not totally naïve. They'll think plenty, and you damn well know it.'

Her voice rose and he said coldly, 'Don't get hysterical, please. After the day I've had—trying to salvage something out of your latest display of incompetence—a hysterical shrew is the very last thing I——'

'After the day *you've* had!' She clutched her hands together, fighting for control. 'I'm the one who was humilated in front of the entire secretarial department, remember. And if I give up my job they'll think I've had a fit of the sulks—or, even worse, that it's safe now for me to show myself for what I am.'

'And what precisely is that?'

'A tarty little desk clerk on the make. I set out to get Tyler Brennan, and now that he's safely hooked I can just sit back and——' unbidden, his words on that magic morning after their marriage came back, so that the desolation almost overwhelmed her '—let you cover me with jewels.'

'Shut up, damn you!' Tyler's bunched hands lifted and for one horrifying moment she thought he was going to strike her. But then he jammed them into his pockets and stood breathing deeply, only that angry flush along his cheekbones warning her into silence.

'I really do not give a. . .' she flinched at the crude obscenity '. . .what my staff think. But if they think anything it'll be the truth—that you've gone the way of any other Brennan employee who couldn't match up to the demands of the job.'

'Oh.' The faint gasp was wrenched from her, the cruel words hurting far more than any physical blow.

'And let me put you right on one other thing. You are not giving up your job, as you choose to put it. You're fired!'

CHAPTER TEN

'FIRED?' Sherry gaped at Tyler, stunned. How could he do this to her? How could he be so heartless? Every fibre of her wanted to crumple on to the floor in front of him, to beg for her job—or at least to say, look what you've done to me. But still that little steel thread of pride kept her backbone upright.

'I don't ever remember seeing my terms of employment,' she said in a tight little voice. 'Perhaps you could kindly inform me how many weeks' notice I have to work out.'

'For heaven's sake!' he exclaimed. 'You don't need to work out any notice.'

'Oh, of course, I was forgetting. You make up the rules as you go along—entirely to suit yourself—don't you?' Her voice was bitter. 'But at least I'm going in tomorrow to clear my desk, to leave everything neat and tidy for my fortunate successor.'

'I've just told you,' his tone was even more clipped, 'there's no need for you to come into the office again—and that's final.'

'You know something, Tyler? You really are a ruthless swine.'

'If you say so,' he agreed, though not at all pleasantly.

'Yes, I do say so. Oh, I know I've made some stupid mistakes lately—mainly because I haven't been feeling well—and, believe me, no one regrets them more than

I do. But the great Tyler Brennan can't stand weakness in others, can he?'

He went to break in, but she swept on. Recently, with Tyler the way he'd been, she'd had to learn pretty fast to bite back, or risk being eaten alive, and now, on top of that, her anger and her hurt were driving her on.

'I'm only surprised you've waited so long. Surely, just one mistake should have been enough? Or you could easily have manufactured one, as you're obviously so anxious to get rid of me.'

She stopped on a little gasp as the full terrible import of her words struck her like a savage blow in the face.

'Oh, for——' Tyler snapped off the words. 'Stop being so bloody melodramatic.' Rolling his eyes heavenwards, he sank down on to the sofa. '*Why* do women always have to over-react to everything?'

'Yes, we always do, don't we? And goodness knows, you must have had more than your fair share of the experience. What a shame, Tyler—I'm sorry to be making such a fuss about *such* an unimportant trifle, but don't worry, I won't mention it again.' And, putting her chin in the air, she stalked past him.

'Where are you going?'

'To the kitchen, of course. Well, that's where I belong, isn't it?'

When he swore again, she remarked sweetly, 'Obscenity is the sign of a limited vocabulary,' and walked on towards the kitchen, head high.

She had just reached the door, when an angry exclamation stopped her in her tracks. She turned, to see the sofa cushion pushed aside, and Tyler holding up the astrology book. Oh, no, of all the times——

'What the hell's this?' He thrust the book towards her and she felt the guilty colour rising in her cheeks.

'Oh, nothing.' Somehow she managed a careless smile. 'I bought it this——'

'I've *told* you—stop wasting your time with this junk.'

'It is *not* junk.'

'I suppose you'll be telling me next that the real reason I'm firing you is because you're a Piscean and I'm a Gemini.'

'I may do just that,' she replied defiantly.

'Perhaps this is all that's wrong with you.' He flung the book aside in exasperation. 'For heaven's sake, Sherry, get your head out of the stars and come back down to the real world.'

When he appeared in the kitchen ten minutes later, Sherry was washing salad at the sink. Out of the corner of her eye, she saw him come in, lean and athletic in his black tracksuit—her stomach muscles contracted painfully for a moment—and pick up his running shoes from behind the door.

He stood somewhere behind her, jingling his car keys softly, but she refused to allow herself to turn round.

'Don't wait for me. I'll be late,' he said in an almost normal tone. 'I'm—er—going to Santa Monica to run. Bye.'

She muttered a 'Bye' then stood rigid as he went out, closing the door, and for several minutes after that. Then, like a lifeless puppet whose strings had been tugged, she roused suddenly and ran back through to the sitting-room.

Standing on tiptoe, she peered down through the

window at the parking area five floors below. Tyler had just emerged—she saw him standing by his sleek navy blue Jaguar coupé, which was parked alongside the pink custom-built Mini he'd had delivered for her, gift-wrapped, two days after they'd touched down in Los Angeles. As she watched, he unlocked his car, hurled his sports bag on to the back seat then got in, reversed at high speed, roared off across the car park rounded a bend and disappeared.

Only then did she draw a long, shuddering breath. She felt the angry tension of the last hour draining out of her, leaving her weak and floppy, like a sawdust-filled puppet. Hastily, she crossed to the sofa and sank down into it. She stared at the opposite wall, her eyes heavy with unshed tears—tears that still ached to be shed but which she fiercely pushed back.

The one consolation in all this, she told herself miserably, was that Tyler's rejection of her was all because of her disasters at work. And yet—and yet, was that really so? She realised that beneath the anger and the hurt of her reaction there had lain a very real terror—a terror which now, for the first time, she let herself take out and look at full in the face.

A PA who'd failed him—was it really so different for a wife? And if Tyler could discard her as his PA with such casual cruelty, surely he could in the future just as easily dispose of an unwanted wife. . .

Her eyes strayed to the book he'd tossed aside. *Your Stars—Your Personality*. . . Had the Gemini factor in Tyler's personality already clicked into action, ticking like a time bomb to explode one day soon and anni-hilate their marriage?

Automatically she bent forward to pick up the book

and glimpsed something shiny by the sofa leg. Kneeling down, she reached underneath and pulled out a gold cufflink then sat back, holding it in her hand. Tyler's cufflink—he'd been looking for it for days. The last time he'd worn it was to that dinner party last week, and when they'd got home——

She closed her eyes to try and shut out the images but her mind would not relent. She'd wandered into the sitting-room, and he'd followed her in, taken her in his arms and—right here—made love to her, shedding both their clothes with a furious urgency which had left them clutching one another, shaken almost beyond bearing.

All at once, Sherry put her head down on her arms and heard a whimper, as if from a small animal in great pain. But she mustn't let herself give way like this. Forcing herself to her feet, her eyes dry as dust, she went back to the kitchen, prepared a simple meal for herself and sat on the sofa with the tray on her lap, untasted, watching TV, programme after programme which she did not see. . .

It was very late when Tyler returned. She lay rigid in bed, watching the light under the bedroom door, listening to him move quietly around the kitchen, then the bathroom. Finally, as the door opened, she waited.

Surely now he would whisper, 'Sherry, are you awake?' He would take her in his arms, tell her he was sorry and make love to her, so that for them both the bitter words and recriminations would be swept away in a torrent of passion—as all her previous mistakes and misdeeds had been.

But he only eased back the duvet, slid soundlessly into the king-sized bed beside her and turned on to his side. Her hand tensed momentarily to touch him, but even as it moved she caught it back and lay motionless, her eyes tightly closed.

Almost immediately, Tyler began to breathe deeply and evenly. She listened to his regular, unforced breathing and thought bitterly, No regrets, no guilty conscience there. But at last, worn out by grief and anger, she too dropped into a heavy sleep. . .

When he arrived in the kitchen next morning she was already there, an unusual amount of make-up in place. It was meant to cover the dark shadows under her eyes, but in fact only served to emphasise her extreme pallor.

As he dropped into a chair opposite her, she slid a coffee-cup towards him and the toast rack.

'Thanks.' He hardly seemed to notice her, busying himself with a sheaf of papers from his case.

Over the rim of her cup, she studied him covertly. He was wearing one of his most expensive suits—in a dark grey slub silk—and a white shirt, still unbuttoned, revealing his strong throat and setting off his tanned face. Unlike her, he hadn't lost his tan, despite spending most of his time recently indoors under artificial lighting.

How handsome he was—the old familiar stab of pain went through her. But how hard, how remote the strong lines of his features, the cool glint of his grey eyes, which she could just glimpse through the shadow of his thick black lashes.

'More toast?' Her voice was almost steady.

'What? Oh, no, thanks.' He glanced up and seemed,

for the first time, to register what she was wearing. He scowled.

'What the hell's that?'

The same half-defiance, half-terror which had gripped her as she dressed caught hold of her now. Crushing down the terror, she said defiantly, 'A sweat-shirt, of course.'

She saw his eyes skim over the black lettering, proudly proclaiming, 'Pisceans of the world unite—you have nothing to lose but your scales!'

She really shouldn't have done it—Tyler was altogether too dangerous for these games. But yesterday's wounds were still raw, and, besides, some self-destructive imp seemed to be luring her helplessly on.

'Is this some kind of gesture, or what?' His voice was unnaturally quiet.

'Well,' she retorted, 'I shan't be needing my business suits from now on, shall I?'

The words ended on a breathy note of barely suppressed terror, but after one more measured look at her Tyler bit back any further response. He drained his cup and set it down.

'More coffee?'

'No, thanks. I'm in a hurry.'

'What's your schedule for today?' she asked brittly.

'I've got a meeting set up with that Sullivan director—I managed to rearrange it for later today.'

'That's good.' Somehow she kept her face expressionless.

He stood up, crossed to the door, then paused. 'And what are you planning for today?'

He'd actually succeeded in sounding as if he cared. 'Oh, don't worry about me,' she snapped. 'I've plenty to occupy me—after all, I've got to spend all afternoon making myself decorative, haven't I?'

His face darkened in an angry scowl but then, with what was obviously a tremendous effort of will, he clamped his mouth tight shut. He just favoured the sweatshirt with one final, level look then said evenly, 'Yes, you have, haven't you?'

As soon as she heard the front door close, she flopped back in her chair, eyes shut. What in heaven's name had got into her—deliberately setting out to provoke him like that? And so very nearly succeeding. Wearily, she passed a hand across her clammy forehead. Oh, lord, she really did feel dreadful—whatever was the matter with her? Reaction from yesterday, and the dangers she'd been dicing with this morning? Yes, but even so, never in her entire life had she felt like this.

Was it Los Angeles? Did it really not suit her? And yet, all around her, in the city, on the beach, in every mall, she saw lithe, tanned, beautiful, young—and not so young—gods and goddesses, radiating vitality. Of course most of them—like Tyler—had probably been born here. He was one of them, while she was an outsider, someone who didn't really belong here and never would, she was sure. Her mouth drooped disconsolately.

Could it be that? Or wasn't it much more likely that it was heartache, and that deep insecurity which lay coiled like an evil dragon at the heart of her relationship with Tyler; the worry that he would in the end prove true to his stars—and untrue to her?

She caught sight of her reflection in the polished steel coffee-pot—strained, her eyes wide and blank, and thought suddenly, with her first really coherent thought in days, Sherry, my girl, this can't go on. You're falling apart at the seams.

A doctor. Yes, that was what she'd do—make an appointment to see Tyler's doctor. Not that a tonic could do much for heartache, but at least if she could talk to someone, tell them how she was losing her grip on things, and how terrified she was that Tyler wouldn't love her any more. . .

Before she could change her mind, she jumped up and hurried through to the sitting-room, found the number and made the appointment—fitted in at midday, and only because she was Tyler Brennan's wife, she acknowledged with a rueful smile as she replaced the receiver.

She glanced at the small gilt clock. Nearly three hours to kill. What should she do? Walk in the park? Go for a drive along the coast in that gift-wrapped Mini that Tyler had bought her just six short weeks ago? She bit hard on her lip as those miserable tears threatened again then, as she turned away, she saw, lying where Tyler had flung it, that book.

She picked it up, put it down, picked it up again. Could she? Dared she? Yes, she could, she thought with another spurt of defiance, driven by an over-whelming need to *know*.

She sat down and flicked through the pages until she found it. 'To work out an individual's birth chart, all you need to know are the precise time, date and place of birth.' Well, Tyler was born in Los Angeles—he'd told her that—and what was it he'd said that first night in his suite in Bristol? Forcing from her mind all other thoughts that that memory aroused, she racked her brains. Yes, that was it 'At three-fifteen a.m. I enter my thirty-sixth year. She'd have to make allowances for the time change from Bristol to Los Angeles, of course, but the tables at the back of the book would do that for her. With a growing sense of daring, she assembled the other items she needed—atlas, calculator, sheets of paper, compass, ruler—spread them out on the dining table and set to work.

Double Gemini!

Sherry stared down at the paper, with its carefully drawn circles and lines. Should she try again? No, she'd already checked, double-checked, then treble-checked, but there was no way round it.

Tyler was a Double Gemini. Not only was it his star sign, but the Gemini constellation had been in the ascendancy at the hour of his birth. She gnawed her lip with dismay. With eleven other constellations to choose from, why, oh, why had those heavenly twins conspired to be in the wrong place at the wrong time?

With a plummeting heart she forced herself to turn on in the book to the character readings. . . Gemini. . . Double Gemini. She read down the page, her eyes darkening with horror, then slammed the book shut and thrust it away from her. But the words still danced up and down behind her eyes.

The trickiest sign in the whole galaxy. Double Geminis have all the Gemini qualities, only in two-fold measure. There's plenty going for them: they're dynamic, physically vibrant, go-getting, likely to be highly successful in business or anything else they turn their hands to.

But then there's a down side. Projects are likely to be taken up with tremendous enthusiasm but then discarded with equal speed as the Gemini low boredom threshold is reached—and nowhere more so than in love. The Double Gemini lover will sweep you off your feet, but is soon likely to prove fickle, changeable in the extreme, as any romantic ties, especially marriage, rapidly turn to prison chains.

They are quite capable of running two relationships at once and this, coupled with their mile-wide ruthless streak, adds up to: Double Gemini—Double Timer—Double Trouble. Don't say you haven't been warned!'

Stark terror clutched at Sherry's heart. She'd been right. Tyler *was* tired of her, bored with their marriage. How long would it be before he began 'running two relationships'? A mistress. . . The word screeched in her brain and, rocking to and fro in misery, she moaned softly, 'Oh, what shall I do?'

But then from somewhere—maybe from way across the Atlantic—came faintly the voice of the old, sensible Sherry. Oh, come on, please. Letting your trust in Tyler be shattered by a few silly words in a book? You know something, Sherida? You are making a fool of yourself, my girl, a real class-one fool.

Of course she was. If she ever confessed to Tyler what she'd just done—not that she'd dare to, of course—he'd despair of her completely. Smiling shamefacedly at her folly, she stood up and, taking hold of the book and Tyler's birth chart between finger and thumb as though they were both somehow grubby, she went through into the bedroom, dropped them into

her dressing-table drawer and began to get ready for
her appointment. . .

Sherry let herself into the apartment and, dropping her
bag on to the table, stood staring into space, her hands
limply at her sides. Finally, she roused herself. She
must have something to eat—not that she was in the
least hungry, but somehow she must force something
down.

Rapidly assembling a round of cottage cheese sand-
wiches, tomato salad, an apple and then, as an after-
thought, a glass of milk, she carried them into the
sitting-room and sank down on to the sofa, looking
around her, still slightly dazed.

Apart from some petals which had dropped from
one of the white chrysanthemums in the jug in the
fireplace the room looked just the same, not altered a
hair's breadth since she'd left it. And yet—everything
was altered, forever, because she was expecting a baby.

'I'm carrying Tyler's child.' She said it aloud softly,
and felt a warm glow inside her. Tyler's child——

Ah, but how will Tyler react? A chill voice, cold and
distinct, was in her ear. Won't it be just one more
prison chain to hold him down?

Don't start that again, she told herself fiercely. Of
course if won't. He'll understand now why I made all
those stupid mistakes—and it will bring us together
again.

Maybe—but would you really want him tied to you
just because of your child. . .?

Desperate to drown that insidious voice, Sherry leapt
to her feet and switched on the television. A quiz show
was just ending and she watched, barely taking it in, as

the contestants, waving and smiling broadly, were borne away on a revolving stage. Then, after the commercials had washed over her, the early afternoon news began.

Peace talks in the latest trouble spot, set against yet more scenes of senseless violence—in a reflex action, she put the palm of her hand protectively against her abdomen. . . two airliners in a near-miss over New York. . . tennis from Dallas. . . Wall Street midday prices. . . And now the local news. . . a bank raid in downtown Los Angeles—an eye-witness being interviewed, in the background a patrol car, siren wailing softly, and——

Sherry set the glass down violently so that some of the milk slopped almost unnoticed over her hand. Then she sank on to her knees in front of the TV set. Only when the item ended and she switched off, her hand still unsteady, did she think, I should have pressed the video recorder switch. Perhaps it wasn't Tyler. If I could just see that clip again, I'd realise that it was someone who didn't even look like him.

Oh, please, Sherry. That cold little voice sounded pained. Don't try to pretend—you saw your husband, walking past on the opposite pavement, his arm round that beautiful redhead, smiling and so wrapped up in her that he probably wouldn't have noticed if a dozen hooded thugs had burst out of the bank, guns blazing.

Who was she? One of his 'relationships' from way back, now being revived? Or maybe not from way back. His new PA perhaps—already lined up—in which case he really had manufactured that final row and her dismissal.

Sherry sat huddled there for a long time, fingernails

picking compulsively at a loose thread in the carpet, but otherwise quite motionless, though inside she felt as though she were being swept helplessly to and fro on an enormous ocean tide.

Her happiness, that feeling she'd had that until she met Tyler she'd only ever been half alive—had it only lasted those few short months? She frowned in the effort to remember. That fatal night in Bristol—she'd been reading her horoscope, hadn't she? Her face crumpled up with pain and she thought, Well, Madame Arcadia, you were right about the exciting new job, money, travel—just a pity you forgot to mention the punchline. Heartbreak.

But she didn't have to stay and watch her own humiliation at first hand. Before the thought crystallised in her mind, she was on her feet and walking towards the bedroom. She'd go home, home to Bristol, where the choisya and the witch-hazel would be in bloom in her tiny garden.

And then she stopped dead. What in heaven's name was she playing at? Oh, she knew perfectly well what she was doing—she was acting out, for the third time in her life, the role of the Piscean victim. Keeling over, hauling up the white flag without even the semblance of a fight, giving up the thing that she cared most for in this world—Tyler's love.

He *had* loved her—she was certain of that—he'd meant every word he'd said on their honeymoon. And now—her fingers curled around her stomach—there was that tiny speck of life, the baby. Surely, with his child——But no. She was not going to use this baby as a weapon. She would win him back herself, with the only weapon she had, the only weapon she'd ever had with Tyler.

With a rapidly beating heart, she went through to the bedroom, sat down at the dressing-table and began to plan her campaign.

CHAPTER ELEVEN

TYLER was late.

Sherry had almost given up asking herself if he was coming home at all when the front door opened. As she heard him walk into the sitting-room her hand, clutching the hairbrush, stilled and her heart began to gyrate wildly. How would he react—would his lips merely curl in contempt at her pitiful little attempt?

How could she possibly have imagined that she could compete with that glamorous redhead?

She made a move as though to leap up from the dressing-table stool, but then sank back. It was too late to back off now.

She heard him pause at the dining alcove, clearly taking in the beautifully laid table, the candles, the flowers and the lovely old Worcester dinner service which his father had presented to her as a belated wedding gift.

Then he appeared in the bedroom doorway.

'H-hello, Tyler.' She did not turn; their eyes met in the mirror.

He made no effort to come in, just lounged against the doorframe, arms folded, taking in every inch of the shocking-pink lace dress which he liked so much, with its narrow shoe-string straps and low-cut bodice which revealed the shadowed tops of her breasts.

'You're looking very—decorative,' he said at last.

'Thank you.' Well, you didn't set out to seduce your husband in jeans and a tatty T-shirt, did you?

'The table looks—pretty decorative, as well,' he went on laconically. 'Is this a private celebration, or can anyone join in?'

'I'm afraid not.' She managed a regretful smile. 'Only my husband.' But then, at the expression in his eyes, she hurried on, 'I—er—thought I'd do lobster thermidor, followed by fresh peaches. In white wine, of course.' Their eyes met in the mirror again.

'Lobster thermidor. Hmmm. I seem to remember hearing some place that lobster doubles as an aphrodisiac—something to do with the zinc content, perhaps.'

'So people say,' she agreed blandly.

She finished smoothing her hair, set down the brush and picked up her pearls, the gorgeous triple strand of black Polynesian pearls which Tyler had bought her on their last day in Tahiti. Very deliberately, she held them out to him.

'Will you do these for me, please? I can never manage the clasp.'

'Of course.'

He straightened up, came over to her and took the pearls. With one hand he brushed her hair aside, then slid them round her throat and deftly hooked them together.

'Thank you.' Now that the moment had come, her voice sounded alarmingly husky.

She stood up and, half turning, smoothed the lace dress down over her hips with a slow gesture which was a blatant sexual provocation. Then, equally slowly, she put up her hands and began unbuttoning his jacket. When she had finished she eased it down off his shoulders, freeing his arms from the sleeves with a little shake, then tossed it on to the floor in an expensive heap. Raising her hands to his tie, she started to undo it, frowning slightly as the knot jammed. Their faces were very near—she could feel his warm breath on her cheek, and the colour rose slightly in her face.

The tie joined the jacket, then she moved on to his white shirt. Tyler was still playing the game her way—he had stood absolutely motionless all the time, just raising his arms a fraction for her to remove his jacket, and he still stood without moving a muscle. Only as her fingers went to the top button of his shirt, then gradually moved down, did she feel from behind his chest wall his heart pounding against his ribs.

He held his wrists perfectly still, as one after the other she removed the sapphire cufflinks and threw them down on to the dressing-table. Then she slid him out of his shirt, her own heartbeat picking up speed as her fingers brushed across the satin-smooth tanned torso.

She knelt down at his feet, undid his laces and when he lifted each foot in turn took off his shoes, then socks. Now only his trousers remained. Drawing a deep breath to steady the flutterings in her throat and chest, she put up her hands to his waistband, revelling in the feel of his hard, taut muscles.

And then at last he moved, putting a hand over hers.

'Before we—er—go any further,' he asked in a silky purr, 'what about the lobster?'

'The lobster can wait,' she said, and undid the button at his waist. . .

*   *   *

Sherry raised her hand and softly brushed his mouth with a butterfly-fingertips kiss. Tyler opened his eyes, smiled then caught her hand and pressed his lips to the palm.

'Tch, tch.' Over her hand he shook his head in teasing reproof. 'I don't know what the world's coming to—shameless young women making love to their own husbands.'

She pouted. 'Oh, dear—don't you approve?'

He slanted her a slow, wicked smile. 'Come here, sweetie, and I'll show you if I approve or not.'

'No—no, Tyler.' She was laughing, struggling helplessly as he pulled her across the bed into his arms. 'I must get dinner. Oh!'

She felt something cold on her stomach, looked down and gave a little wail. 'Oh, no, my pearls—my beautiful pearls.'

Some time, in the passion of their lovemaking, the fine clasp must have snapped and now, as she moved, black pearls were sent rolling over the sheet to spill down on to the floor in all directions.

'Well, if you will be so—uh—abandoned,' Tyler remarked.

'Oh, shut up,' she giggled. 'Come and help me look for them.'

Torn between laughter and dismay, and regardless of her total lack of clothing, Sherry was grovelling around on the carpet, picking up pearls. Very leisurely, Tyler eased himself off the bed, slipped on his black kimono and came down on his haunches beside her, then together they combed the floor.

'I think that must be it.' Sherry retrieved one last pearl from under the dressing-table then sat back, looking at the glowing heap on the bed. 'How many were there?'

He lifted one shoulder in a careless shrug. 'Oh, about a hundred and fifty, I should think.'

One hundred and fifty Tahitian pearls. Not for the first time, Sherry shuddered inwardly at the thought of their cost, but then she caught Tyler's eye and they both dissolved into helpless laughter.

'Don't worry, honey,' he said at last. 'I'll take them into town tomorrow and get them restrung.'

Reaching for his jacket, which still lay on the floor, he extracted a handkerchief, shook it out of its folds and, laying it on the bed, started piling pearls on to it.

'I'll go and get dinner.' Sherry half got to her feet but he put a detaining hand on her wrist.

'I'll do it—you stay here.'

'Please—I want to.'

She bent foward and, aching with love for him, kissed his cheek softly then got up to retrieve her clothes.

'OK, you win,' he said. 'Now, I'll put these away safely for tonight.'

Sherry sat on the bed, pulling her dress over her head as he gathered together the corners of the handkerchief and went across to the dressing-table. Leaning forward, she did up the zip of her dress, only half aware of Tyler opening the drawer, dropping in the bundle of pearls. There was a faint crackle of paper.

'What the devil's this?'

Alerted by an intangible something in his voice, she swivelled round to see him standing over her, holding——

A faint gasp was torn from her. She tried to meet his eye but failed miserably.

'It's—it's that book,' she stammered.

'I can read, thanks.' All the remaining warmth had gone from his voice. 'I thought I told you not to mess with this stuff.'

Angrily, he flicked it open then as she watched, with a feeling of sick doom, bent to retrieve the folded paper which had fluttered out. He opened it, read aloud 'Double Gemini', then, with one glance at her, his mouth closed like a rat trap and she saw his eyes skimming rapidly down the closely written page.

Finally he raised his eyes once more to hers. His voice was dangerously quiet. 'I know—don't ask me how—that this,' he brandished the paper in her face, 'is something to do with all this.' His contemptuous gesture encompassed their clothes, abandoned all over the floor. 'For the last time, Sherry, if you know what's good for you, stop psychoanalysing me like some damn shrink.'

'But it's all true.' Somehow she pulled herself together. 'Every word of it. You're a Double Gemini. So——'

'Oh? And what's that, whatever it is, supposed to make me?' The open sneer in his voice flicked her on the raw.

'It's not *supposed* to make you anything. It makes you twice as fickle, twice as two-timing, twice as——'

'Oh, for——'

'False. And every word of it's true.' For at least an hour she'd forgotten the scene on the TV screen, which she'd thought she'd remember till her dying day. Now the bitterness of betrayal swept through her like acid bile. 'Particularly true in your case.'

'And what the hell do you mean by that?' He was standing over her, his hands jammed hard into his kimono pockets as if to prevent himself from seizing her by the throat. 'Just what's going on in that tiny warped mind of yours?'

Sherry sucked in her breath. How dared he? She'd intended to be cool and laid-back, to be discreet, and then she wouldn't blow her chance. But his brazen attack fuelled the bitterness.

'Don't bother to come the innocent with me, Tyler.' She leaned back against the padded bedhead. 'I saw you—or rather saw you both—on TV this afternoon.'

'TV?'

'Yes—that bank raid. They were interviewing an eyewitness and you happened to walk by. Oh, you didn't see the camera—you were much too engrossed in that redhead.' She said the word fiercely, as though spitting it out of herself, then glared up at him. 'Well, go on—deny it.'

'Is that what we Double Gemini two-timers are supposed to do? Enlighten me please, darling.'

'Y-yes.' There was something about the way he spoke which threw her off balance. 'Yes, it is.'

'Well, sorry, but I've not the slightest intention of denying it.' And as she stared at him, shocked beyond belief, he dropped down on to the bed, arms folded. 'You're quite right. I have spent the afternoon with a redhead—a delicious, gorgeous redhead.'

As hope finally died in her, the pain came to take its place. He wasn't even going to pretend. In that case—

Sherry hardly knew she had moved, until Tyler reached a hand across to detain her. Without seemingly exerting more than a fraction of his strength, he dragged her across the bed, struggling frantically, and held her pinioned in his arms.

'L-let me go, damn, you,' she panted, glowering at him through her hair. 'You—you—I'm leaving you.'

'Oh, no, you're not,' he said very quietly. And bending towards her he nibbled softly at her left ear. Immediately, the old treacherous sensations rippled through her and, furious with herself, she fought to pull away.

'If you think I'm letting you behave like—like——'

'A two-timing Gemini,' he said in her ear.

'You're absolutely mistaken. I'm off.'

'Jealous, are you?'

'Of course I am—no, certainly not!' she yelled at him, and disbelievingly saw him give that smug panther's smile.

But then the smile faded and lifting his hand he flicked away the tear which hung quivering on her lashes. 'You really don't need to be, my darling.'

'No?' She gulped.

'No. You see, my sweet, that redhead who inadvertently strayed on to camera with me is Patsy Sullivan.'

Sherry almost leapt ouf of his arms with shock. 'Of Sullivan Airlines? But—but you were meeting their manager director.'

'Mmmm, that's right.' Tyler was watching her face with interest.

'But she's a woman.'

He clicked his tongue. 'That's a remarkably sexist comment, Mrs Brennan.'

'Yes, well——' she began defensively. 'Of an airline?'

'If you recall, my meeting was with the *joint* managing director. She's the marketing and sales half of the team, and her husband—she and Brett have been happily married for fifteen years, by the way—runs the operational side of their business.'

'And you weren't. . .' She hesitated.

'Propositioning her?' Tyler grinned. 'Nobody, but nobody propositions Mrs Patsy Sullivan, my sweet. She's one tough cookie, that one. Although maybe I was using,' he gave her a sly look, 'just a little of my Gemini charm. And in case you're wondering, it seems to have worked. We've got a Brennan-Sullivan link-up—I've called a special board meeting for tomorrow to discuss it.'

What a fool she'd made of herself. Sherry hung her head and said in a very small voice, 'I'm sorry.' But there was still one tiny thing worrying her, needing to be cleared up. 'Would you like a wife like that, Tyler?' She spoke so softly that he had to bend to hear her.

'You mean a glamorous businesswoman who sets up multi-million-dollar deals, jets round the world at an hour's notice, and runs a house, husband and three sons with military efficiency?'

'Something like that,' she whispered.

'No,' he said firmly. 'I'd far rather my wife left all that hassle to me. That's if she has no objections, of course.'

Almost inaudibly Sherry murmured, 'I thought you didn't love me any more.'

Tyler's arms tightened round her, but he only said, 'Because I've been a bit—moody, you mean?'

Her lips twitched slightly. 'Just a bit.'

'Well, OK—I've been a total bastard. I'm sorry, my darling,' his voice was ragged, 'I've made your life an utter misery. It's just—there have been so many problems the last few weeks. And also—I guess I have to admit it—I do not like being hog-tied to my work. Since we got back to LA I've heard the door of the Brennan prison cage close behind me with a clang, and I don't much care for it.'

He gave her a rueful smile. 'Maybe there's something, at least, in this star signs business—about Geminis, I mean. I do get restless, impatient, bored and I guess I do over-react more than somewhat when I feel trapped. By LA—or my work,' he went on quickly, as her mouth tightened momentarily, 'but never, ever, I promise you, my darling, by you.'

She could feel the happiness, and the relief, surging through her as he went on, with a self-deprecating grin, 'But as for this Double Gemini rule, well, surely you know me well enough by now to be certain that when Tyler Brennan sees a rule he breaks it. And anyway, how about you? You're a Piscean—right?'

'Yes—you know that.'

'Pisceans are victims—right?'

'Sometimes,' she muttered.

'Pisceans are poor, downtrodden slaves—right?'

She smothered a laugh. 'Well—perhaps.'

'Pisceans never fight back—right?'

This time she laughed out loud. 'Of course not.'

'So—just what have you been doing for the past hour and a half,' he gave her a meaning look which turned her cheeks peony-pink, 'if not fighting back—

fighting like crazy to win back your husband from that oh, so luscious redhead?'

When she made no reply, he said, 'Because that's what all this,' he casually ran his finger along the top of her lace dress, '*was* all about, isn't it?'

She nodded reluctantly.

'Well, then,' he wound up triumphantly, 'if you can break every rule in the book, so can I. And anyway, if that doesn't convince you, didn't they ever teach you at school what two minuses make?'

She stared up at him, bewildered by this sudden change of tack.

'Er—I can't remember.'

'Two minuses make a plus, of course. So—a Double Gemini, a double two-timer, makes the most loving, faithful husband ever. Didn't you know that?'

'Oh, Tyler.' And happy tears made her eyes like stars.

'And that reminds me.' He loosed his hold of her and stood up. 'Wait here.'

He was back almost at once with a sheaf of papers. 'Want to know why I went to Santa Monica last night?'

'Well, to train,' she said wonderingly.

'True, but I could have done that perfectly well three blocks from home, my little dumbo. I went for these.' And he tossed the papers into her lap.

She picked up the top sheet and saw that it contained house details from a real estate firm. As she looked from it to Tyler, her eyes enormous, he sat down beside her again, putting his arm round her.

'I know you're not happy in this apartment. No. . .' as she tried to protest. 'And I'm not now. Oh, it suited me well enough as a bachelor pad, but I want something special for us. Something like this, perhaps.'

Extracting one of the papers he held up a picture of a pleasant-looking, old pink-painted house, with a veranda and set in spacious gardens.

'I remember how much you liked Santa Monica that weekend we went there. Think it might suit you?'

'Yes—please.' It was all she could trust herself to say.

'It'll be something for us to come back to when we've been off on our next island-hopping trip.'

'Mmmm,' she said non-committally. 'Although I may not always come with you on those.'

'You won't?' He looked dismayed for a moment, but then added quickly, 'No, well, that'll be up to you, my sweet. And whenever you don't come, you'll always be here when I get back.'

He took her hand in his and began stroking his thumb round and round in her palm. 'I know it sounds selfish, but that's what I need from you—a still, calm centre in my life, which I can't seem to make for myself. That's if you don't mind, of course.' He shot her a lop-sided smile.

'You know I don't,' she replied tremulously.

Of course she couldn't shackle him—a high-flying Gemini should never have his wings clipped to keep him out of the air which was his natural element. But she'd always be there—his rock, his anchor—whenever he touched down on terra firma.

He lifted her hands and kissed the knuckles one by one. 'Oh, Sherry,' he murmured. 'I've been such a swine to you.'

Suddenly he gave an exclamation. 'Good grief, I almost forgot.'

Dropping her hands he leapt up once more and made for the door. 'Close your eyes.'

She heard a rustle, then Tyler's voice saying, 'This is why I was late this evening. I had to collect him.'

Sherry opened her eyes. The bear, honey-brown, was standing on the floor in front of her, four feet tall on his cream suede paws.

'He's got a name.' Grinning like a Cheshire cat, he pointed to the leather collar round the bear's fat neck, with its gilt name tag.

She took hold of it, turned it over then, as the letters blurred in front of her, she read shakily, 'Albert Edward.'

As she bit her lip, Tyler said, 'Hey, no tears, please.' He laughed, then added, 'I seem to remember saying something like that all those million years ago in Bristol.'

'Thank you, Tyler.' She was almost too overwhelmed to speak. 'He—he's lovely.'

'Well, he's intended as an apology. I've been so vile to you—home here, and most of all at work. And talking of work,' his voice all at once sounded almost uncertain, 'that board meeting tomorrow—do you think you can possibly make it?'

'But you——'

'Fired you? Yes I know. But even the great Tyler Brennan can make mistakes.' He pulled a face, half comical, half wry. 'I've missed you like hell today. I was intending to ask my father's old PA to take over— and no, she isn't a glamorous redhead.' He gave her an irrepressible grin. 'She's fussed over me for the last twenty years. But if you think you can put up with me, will you come back?'

'Oh, Tyler, I'd have loved to. But I'm sorry—I don't think I ought to. You see, I wouldn't be able to stay very long.' She looked down so that he shouldn't see just yet the glow in her eyes. 'I haven't been feeling well, so I went to the doctor this morning and——'

'And?' he interrupted, seizing her by the arms, his fingers biting into her flesh. 'You're not ill, are you Sherry? Is that what you're trying to tell me?'

'No. I'm having a baby,' she said softly, and gave him a luminous smile.

'A—baby.' Tyler repeated the word stupidly, but still it didn't seem to register. He went on staring at her, and then she saw the shock darken in his eyes. 'Are you sure?'

Wasn't he pleased? He certainly didn't look pleased.

'Y-yes,' she faltered. 'It's early days, of course, but Dr Weinstein is quite sure.'

'But how? Oh, lord.' He ran his fingers distractedly through his hair. 'What an idiot thing to say.'

'Well, women do sometimes have them, you know,' she said, still slightly uncertain.

'A baby,' he repeated, then. 'Oh, my darling girl. I'm so glad,' then finally, 'Oh, Sherry, what a swine I've been to you.'

His voice was husky with remorse and she quickly put her hand out to him. 'It doesn't matter—really.'

'I'll go and get dinner.' He tensed to get up, but she restrained him.

'No, please. I'm not hungry.'

'Yes, you must eat. You've hardly eaten anything for days. Now, put your feet up.'

'Oh, no,' she protested, laughing. 'I'm not an invalid—the baby isn't due till the end of July. I will eat later, I promise,' as he scowled, 'but I'm just not hungry now.'

'In that case. . .' He drew her into his arms, but then backed off hastily. 'Am I allowed to. . .? I mean——'

'Of course. If you really want to,' she said demurely.

'In that case. . .' He flopped back down on to the bed, one arm thrown behind his head. 'I forgot to tell you, there's just one rule I never break.'

'Oh, and what's that?'

'A Double Gemini never does anything in singles. So, my sweet,' he gave her a slow, languorous smile which set her pulses beating feverishly, then reached for her with a lazy hand, 'come here.'

CHAPTER TWELVE

'Mrs Brennan.' The nurse spoke softly. 'Your husband is here to see you.'

Sherry, still drowsy from the anaesthetic, opened her eyes and saw Tyler, his arms full of pink carnations, coming towards her.

He stood beside the bed looking down at her, very pale, his face still drawn from the night's trauma.

'Hi.' He gave her a very wan smile.

'I'll take the flowers, shall I, Mr Brennan?'

This nurse was obviously used to dealing with punch-drunk new fathers.

'Thank you, Tyler.' Sherry smiled up at him. 'They're lovely.'

'Actually, they're from Dad.'

'How is he?'

He pulled a face. 'Fine now. We both are.' Although he certainly didn't look it. 'He wanted to come down here last night but I wouldn't let him.'

'I should think not.' She tried, unsuccessfully, to sound severe.

'After all,' he went on wryly, 'one Brennan wearing out the carpet in the waiting-room and snarling at every unsuspecting individual who came through the door was more than enough, I should think.'

He managed a very shaky laugh, then his face twisted. 'Oh, Sherry—when they made me leave you,

I didn't know what to do. I was nearly going off my head out there.'

He sat down on the extreme edge of the bed, stroking her cheek softly, as though she were made of cut glass, then asked remorsefully, 'Was it very dreadful?'

'No—not at all. And anyway——' she gave him a tender smile '—it was worth it, don't you think?'

Her gaze strayed towards the two cribs beside the bed, from which he had so far resolutely turned away his eyes.

'Would you like to hold your sons, Mr Brennan?' The nurse was back.

'Well, I'm not——'

For the second time in a few hours, Sherry saw stark terror in her husband's eyes, but then he obediently took a small white cocoon in the crook of each arm.

She watched him as, very gingerly, he held the sleeping babies and looked down at the two perfect miniature replicas of himself, each complete with thatch of black hair and tiny, determined Brennan jaw, and at the expression on his face she felt her heart-strings twist inside her.

Very gently he stroked a little red hand, and the fingers closed tightly around his finger. He looked up at her, his grey eyes bright, and gave a rather off-centre smile.

'Clever Sherry.'

She shook her head. 'Clever Tyler. After all, it's your grandmother and great-grandmother who were both twins, isn't it?'

When the babies, sucking frantically on their blankets, had been replaced in their cribs, he took her hand, raising it to his lips and kissing each fingertip in turn.

'Thank you, my darling,' he said, with a husky catch in his voice.

'I think you ought to go home and get some sleep,' she murmured.

He yawned hugely. 'Yeah, maybe I will at that. What a night.' He rolled his eyes. 'First you letting on you didn't feel well on the freeway halfway home from Dad's, then Doc Weinstein deciding he'd have to induce the birth a month early——Oh, good grief!'

He stopped abruptly with a shout of laughter. 'It's only just registered. A month early! Don't you realise what you've done, my sweet?'

When Sherry shook her head in bewilderment, he went on, 'Today is June the nineteenth. So—I'm afraid you have just produced Gemini twins. Surely there must be something in that astrology book of yours about Gemini twins?'

'I don't know.' Her laugh was more than half horrified. Two more Gemini males?

Tyler pulled a rueful face. 'However will you manage?'

The very question she was asking herself. 'Oh, I expect I'll cope—with great difficulty,' she said teasingly.

'Well, next time I promise you we'll time things better. We'll have Piscean girl twins—I seem to recall that Piscean females are supposed to be docile and submissive to their lords and masters, although I've never seen much sign of that myself.'

'Why, you——' She put her hand against his chest

to push him over, but he captured it between his and, turning it palm up, carried it to his lips.

'I promise you one thing, my darling.' Over her hand, his eyes, brimming with love, met hers. 'Your three tame Gemini males will be your slaves forever.'

'Tyler Brennan—tame? Never,' she said, but with a catch in her voice.

Then, as the poignant happiness welled up almost unendurably inside her, she drifted off to sleep, Tyler still holding her hand.

STARGAZING

YOUR STAR SIGN: **GEMINI (May 21–June 20)**

GEMINI is the third sign of the Zodiac, ruled by the planet Mercury and controlled by the element Air. These make you inquisitive, witty, cheerful and—sometimes—inconsistent. Renowned for your dual personality, you tend to be fickle, but being a creature of the moment could be an advantage as you may make note of something today and make it tomorrow's aim!

Socially, Geminis are friendly and natural communicators—you love to chat with people about anything, just to find out what makes them tick. Even though you are a social butterfly and a gracious host, your moody side can see permanence at home restrictive—so your family might have to wait a while for the dust to settle!

Your characteristics in love: Restless and spirited, Gemini do not like to be tied down and partners may find them unreliable, since they are considered to be born flirts. Your twin nature allows you to handle many

185

things at the same time—and that includes lovers!
Nevertheless, you are quick-minded and can talk yourself out of trouble so that partners are left exhausted
by trying to keep up with you!

**Signs which are compatible with you: Leo, Aries,
Libra** and **Aquarius**, while **Taurus, Virgo and
Scorpio** provide you with a challenge. Partners born
under other signs can be compatible, depending on
which planets reside in their Houses of Personality and
Romance.

What is your star-career? Able to juggle many things
in the air at once, Geminis enjoy a great deal of variety
in their work. Employment which involves good com-
munication skills and versatility will attract you, such
as publishing, broadcasting, interpreting, teaching and
counselling.

Your colours and birthstones: Your favourite colours
are bright blue and yellow which are sometimes com-
bined in interiors. Your birthstones are agate; a mu-
table stone found in different colours reflecting the
chameleon-like nature of this mercurial sign and pearl,
a rare gem which is regarded as a symbol of chastity
and purity.

GEMINI ASTRO-FACTFILE

Day of the week: Wednesday
Countries: United States and Wales
Flowers: Lily of the valley and lavender
Food: Chicken and shrimps; Gemini cook on the spur of the moment, often trying unusual or exotic food since variety is the spice of life!
Health: Make sure your nervous energy does not exhaust your body as basic body functions such as eating and sleeping are just as important. Learn to relax more by breathing correctly and treating tension with a massage!

You share your star sign with these famous names:

Paul McCartney
Bob Hope
Clint Eastwood
Mike Gatting
Bob Dylan

Kylie Minogue
Cilla Black
Joan Collins
Priscilla Presley
Kathleen Turner

ZODIAC LOVE MATCH

CALL THE MILLS & BOON
LOVE MATCH HOTLINE

The only service to give you a detailed love analysis of your own star sign and then tell you how romantically compatible you are with the man of your dreams.

If you're interested in hearing how you match up with that special man in your life, or just want to know who would suit you best, all you have to know is your own star sign and that of the man you're interested in hearing yourself matched with.

If you dial the special Love Match 'phone number shown below, we will connect you to Catriona Roberts Wright who will give you an in-depth report on how compatible your two signs are.

CAN YOU BEAR TO WAIT?

DIAL 0898 600 077 NOW

Calls charged 33p per minute cheap rate.
44p per minute at all other times.

Next month's Romances

Each month, you can choose from a world of variety in romance with Mills & Boon. These are the new titles to look out for next month.

A PROMISE TO REPAY Amanda Browning

SHOTGUN WEDDING Charlotte Lamb

SUCH SWEET POISON Anne Mather

PERILOUS REFUGE Patricia Wilson

PASSIONATE BETRAYAL Jacqueline Baird

AN UNEQUAL PARTNERSHIP Rosemary Gibson

HAPPY ENDING Sandra Field

KISS AND SAY GOODBYE Stephanie Howard

SCANDALOUS SEDUCTION Miranda Lee

BACKLASH Elizabeth Oldfield

ANGELA'S AFFAIR Vanessa Grant

WINDSWEPT Rosalie Henaghan

TIGER MOON Kristy McCallum

THE PRICE OF DESIRE Kate Proctor

COUNTRY BRIDE Debbie Macomber

STARSIGN
DARK PASSION Sally Heywood

Available from Boots, Martins, John Menzies, W.H. Smith, Woolworths and other paperback stockists.

Also available from Mills and Boon Reader Service, P.O. Box 236, Thornton Road, Croydon, Surrey CR9 3RU.

MILLS & BOON
STARSIGN ROMANCES

We hope you are enjoying our new 'STARSIGN ROMANCES'. They are a new variation to our contemporary Romance series, and we would like to know what you think about them.

Spend a few minutes telling us your views and we will send you a FREE Mills & Boon Romance as our thank you.

Don't forget to fill in your name and address, so that we know where to send your FREE book!

Please tick the appropriate box for each question. ☑

1 **Have you enjoyed reading the STARSIGN ROMANCES?**

Very Much ☐ Quite a Lot ☐ Not Very Much ☐ Not at All ☐

2 **How many of the STARSIGN ROMANCES have you read?**

1 ☐ 2 ☐ 3 ☐ 4 ☐ 5 ☐ Don't Know ☐

3 **What do you like about the covers for the STARSIGN ROMANCES?**

_____

_____

4 **What do you dislike about the covers for the STARSIGN ROMANCES?**

_____

_____

5 **Do you think enough emphasis is placed on the star signs of the hero and heroine?**

There should be more emphasis ☐
The emphasis is just right ☐
There should be less emphasis ☐

6 In the STARSIGN ROMANCES the star sign of the month, e.g. Aries, alternates between the hero and the heroine.

Do you prefer the hero to be the star sign of the month? ☐
Do you prefer the heroine to be the star sign of the month? ☐
You don't mind either? ☐
You prefer them to alternate? ☐

7 How interested are you in horoscopes?

Very Interested ☐   Not Very Interested ☐
Quite Interested ☐   Not at all Interested ☐

8 Are there any further comments that you would like to make about the STARSIGN ROMANCES?

_____
_____
_____

9 Where do you get your STARSIGN ROMANCES from?

Mills & Boon Reader Service ☐   New from the shops ☐
Other (please specify) ☐

10 Which of the following series do you read?

Mills & Boon: Romances ☐   Best Seller ☐   Temptation ☐
            Medical Romances ☐   Masquerade ☐   Collection ☐
Silhouette: Sensation ☐   Desire ☐   Special Edition ☐
Various: Loveswept ☐   Zebra ☐   None of These ☐

11 What age group are you?

16-24 ☐ 25-34 ☐ 35-44 ☐ 45-54 ☐ 55-64 ☐ 65 plus ☐

DDZ

Thank you for your help. Please send completed form to:
Mills & Boon Reader Service, P.O. Box 236, Croydon, Surrey, CR9 3RU.

Name _____
Address _____
_____ Postcode _____